M000297686

NO WEDDING
FOR OLD MEN

Also by Wendy Delaney

The Working Stiffs Mystery Series

Trudy, Madly, Deeply
Sex, Lies, and Snickerdoodles
There's Something About Marty
You Can't Go Gnome Again
Dogs, Lies, and Alibis

NO WEDDING FOR OLD MEN

A Working Stiffs Mystery
Book 6

Wendy Delaney

NO WEDDING FOR OLD MEN

Copyright © 2019 by Wendy Delaney

All rights reserved. Except as permitted under the U.S. Copyright Act of 1976, no part of this publication may be reproduced, distributed, or transmitted in any form or by any means now known or hereafter invented, or stored in a database or retrieval system, without the prior written permission of the author, Wendy Delaney.

This book is a work of fiction. Names, characters, places, and incidents are the product of the author's imagination or are used fictitiously. Any resemblance to actual persons, living or dead, business establishments, events, or locales is coincidental.

Cover by Lewellen Designs

Printed in the United States of America

First Edition
First Printing, 2019

ISBN-13: 978-0-9986597-1-8
ISBN-10: 0998659711

Sugarbaker Press

To all my friends at Duke's Cafe.
You put the happy in our pie happy hour.

Acknowledgments

All my books are labors of love, but now that I have eight under my belt, it's become obvious to me that some books are more labor-intensive than others. *No Wedding For Old Men* required lots of walking, lots of "what-ifs," and quite a few conversations about "life" to be born, ironically about nine months after the story first took hold in my brain. So many thanks go out to Kathy Coatney and Celeste Deveney. Not once did you ask, "Are you going to write this book or just talk about it?" Wisely, you left that question for me to ask. I sure am glad I finally answered it!

Thanks as always to my "guy stuff" expert, Jeff. Not a role you volunteered for, but you married me, so you've got it, babe!

Jody Sherin, you were with me every step of the way on this book. It turned out to be a long and winding road to publication, but I'm very grateful for all your time and good company.

To "K," my "cop stuff" advisor, I'm so appreciative of your guidance. Without you I would surely go astray.

Elizabeth Flynn, my favorite sock diva and editor, you're teaching me to be a better writer. Thank you!

Lastly, I offer my heartfelt thanks to my dream team of beta-readers and supporters: Heather Chargualaf, Judy Thacker, Deidre Herzog, Lori Dubiel, Susan Cambra, Brandy Lanfair-Jones, Denise Fluhr, Cindy Nelson, Vicki Huskey, Kimber Hungerman, Amber Lassig, Jan Dobbins, Mattie Piela, Jana Buxton, Beth Rosin, Connie Lightner, Brenda Randolph, Christie Marks, Denise Keef, Liz Schwab, and Karen Haverkate. And thank you, Team Delaney! You're all awesome and I'm very grateful to have you with me on this journey.

Chapter One

I HAD THE same problem this Saturday morning that I'd had every weekend since a big black furry dog named Fozzie became my roommate.

A rude awakening from an oversized fur ball who didn't give a rip about his designated human's desire to catch a few extra winks.

"I'm up. I'm up," I told the whimpering alarm clock pawing at my bedroom door.

Rubbing the sleep from my eyes, I reached for my cell phone. I'd hoped to see a text message from my boyfriend, Steve Sixkiller, one of the Chimacam County Search and Rescue team members who had been called out last night.

Nothing. Dang it.

I shivered. Not because I was leaving a nice, warm bed, but because I had the very bad feeling that no news about the man who had gone missing wasn't good news.

After a quick trip to the bathroom, I called Steve's cell, but it went to voice mail after four rings. "Any news? Call me."

When he hadn't responded to my message by the time I returned to my apartment from walking Fozzie around the block, I grabbed my car keys and headed to the one place in town that I could reliably count on for the latest news: my great-uncle Duke's diner.

Since it was Saturday, Duke's Cafe wouldn't be humming with the typical workday crowd, but that was okay. I didn't need them. I needed Lucille Kressey, Duke's longest-tenured waitress, to be working her usual morning shift.

It also wouldn't hurt if the driver of the black and white patrol car I parked next to had stopped by for a breakfast break.

Hector Avocato, Duke's weekend line cook, smiled through the window over the grill and offered me a chin salute as I shut the front door behind me. "*Querida*, what brings you here so early this fine June morning? My irresistible charm, or did you develop a sudden craving for the best apple fritters in town?"

After months of cutting calories to fit into the bridesmaid dress I had to wear in two weeks, the last item on my list of things to do today was to start indulging my sugar cravings. "I'm on the fritter-free menu plan until after my mother's wedding, so it must have been your undeniable charm."

Lucille scowled as she filled the coffee mug in front of the uniformed patrolman sitting alone at the counter. "Charm, right. I bet I know what brings you here."

I didn't want to play my hand too quickly and scare off a potential source, especially since Lucille had set a mug at the seat next to Howie Fontaine like an invitation to join the rookie cop for breakfast.

While she poured me a cup of inky brew, I slid my butt onto the barstool. "Yep, but it doesn't look like

Steve remembered that he and I had a breakfast date this morning." Nor did it look as if I had remembered it prior to this very minute, seeing that I didn't have an ounce of makeup on.

Chewing on a slice of toast, Howie turned to me. "Sorry to be the one to tell you, Charmaine, but he's not gonna make it."

"Would be nice if he'd tell me that." I pulled out my cell phone from my tote and made a show of checking for messages. "I haven't heard a peep out of him since last night."

Howie reached for his coffee. "That's because he's out of range."

That didn't come as any great surprise. Rural Chimacam County wasn't renowned for its cellular coverage. "You talked to him?"

"Left him about an hour ago."

"So you were part of the search team." Also no big surprise. Like Steve, most of the more athletic members of Port Merritt's fourteen-person police department were search and rescue volunteers.

Howie nodded and took a slurp of coffee. "Until it turned into a recovery effort."

Lucille set down the carafe on the scarred lemon-yellow Formica counter separating us and leaned in. "Steve told you who went missing, right?"

"Heck, no." Steve had a long-standing tradition of keeping me out of all the loops not available to the general public. "Who?"

"Ted Skerrett," she said, lowering her voice to a stage whisper.

I mainly knew Ted from waitressing here at Duke's

after moving back to Port Merritt last summer. Nice guy. Good tipper. Also a bit of a flirt, which made the charismatic septuagenarian popular with the ladies.

"Ted Skerrett!" I looked to Howie. "What happened?"

He drained the last of his coffee. "No further comment until the sheriff releases a statement."

"Do you know if anyone reported it to my office?" Because if Ted's body had been recovered, the deputy coroner on call this weekend needed to be notified.

"Yeah. They're probably on their way now."

"To where?"

Howie gave his head a shake. "I don't think the sheriff wants that to become public knowledge just yet."

If I had learned anything during my ten months working as an assistant to the Chimacam County Prosecutor/Coroner, it was that death investigations required coffee. Seeing how I'd probably end up doing a good portion of the legwork on this case come Monday, I thought that I might as well start by supplying the coffee this morning.

That required a *where*, and with Howie reaching for his wallet I needed to present a convincing argument and fast.

I pointed at the carafe steaming at the coffee station behind Lucille. "Could I take all that?"

Lucille stepped aside to let me pull out a stack of to-go cups from under the counter. "Sure, but—"

"Order up," Hector called out with enough volume to send the clear message that he'd like his waitress to get back to work.

She heaved a sigh. "Don't say anything important

until I get back."

I waited for Lucille and her squeaky orthopedic shoes to depart with her order and then turned back to Howie. "Did anyone bring you something to eat while you were there?"

"Someone brought us some sandwiches around midnight, but..."

"I'll take some doughnuts to go with the coffee."

He narrowed his eyes at me. "I don't know if that's a good idea."

Maybe not, but it was the idea I was running with.

"And as a death investigator for the county, I'd better get there as quickly as I can. What's the location?"

Blowing out a breath of resignation, Howie motioned for me to follow him to the cash register, where we could speak without prying ears.

To avoid raising Lucille's suspicion, I took his order ticket and rang it up.

"You know the Gibson Lake area?" he asked, handing me a twenty.

"Yep." It bordered acres of rich timberland that marked the western boundary of the county. The Gibson Lake community was also where, as a body language expert, I'd worked a coroner case last fall.

"North of there on State Route 15 is the Spirit Rim Trail. You should see a couple of sheriffs' vehicles parked near the trailhead."

I dropped his change into his palm. "Got it."

Pocketing his wallet, Howie drilled me with the wary cop glare I'd received from Steve more times than I could count. "You didn't hear that from me."

"I got that too," I said, watching him walk away.

❋

Standing at the trailhead less than an hour later, I was on the receiving end of the same cop glare when I greeted Steve with my box of doughnuts.

He shook me off. "What are you doing here?"

"Duke sent me with doughnuts and coffee when he heard what happened."

"Since Hector is the one behind the grill most Saturdays, I seriously doubt that."

Busted. "Okay, so I took the initiative on behalf of the family business."

"Right." Steve scowled at the row of cars behind me. "How far do I have to walk to get a cup of this allegedly donated coffee?"

I pointed at the coffee station I'd set up on the hood of his pickup, parked next to a white and green sheriff's SUV. "Since you were parked a lot closer than me, I didn't think you'd mind."

"Give me one of those," he said, reaching into the pink bakery box in my hands.

While Steve made his way to my makeshift coffee station, I glanced over at the sheriff's deputy standing guard next to the carved wooden sign marking the trail. "Where's everyone else?"

Chewing, Steve dumped a couple of creamers into one of the paper cups of industrial-strength coffee. "It's just the sheriff's guys now, and they're finishing up with Shondra."

Steve didn't have to elaborate. Having assisted Criminal Prosecutor Shondra Alexander on some of her cases, I knew the former cop to be painstakingly thorough both as an attorney and on the rare occasion when she filled in for the coroner. No doubt she was making everyone with jurisdictional responsibility wait so that she could document the scene before they moved the body.

I also knew how Shondra liked her coffee, so after Steve took off and I spotted the tall black woman in the rain slicker dodging mud puddles on her way down the trail, I sugared a cup and waited for her a few feet from the deputy.

"Are you supposed to be here, Charmaine?" she asked, her gaze piercing me with laser focus. "Because I'm pretty sure that Dispatch didn't also rouse you out of bed to hightail it over here."

"I happened to be at Duke's when the news hit about Mr. Skerrett."

"I swear, people in these parts can't keep their dang mouths shut. At least tell me there's an apple fritter in that box."

"There should be a couple." Only because I had put the bakery box in the back seat of my car so that I couldn't reach them while I was driving.

"Good, I'm starved," Shondra said, charging past me at a steady clip despite the weight of the black duffle bag she was carrying.

I took that as my cue to follow Shondra to her Mercedes SUV, where I watched her pop the rear hatch and stow the duffle bag—not so affectionately referred to as the "bag of death" by most of the staff.

"I assume you're done here?" I asked when she started dousing her hands with liquid sanitizer.

"Considering I should be sleeping in right now, I'm so done."

"Any conclusion as to the cause of death?"

Raising her hands in front of her like a doctor scrubbed for surgery, Shondra slanted me a glance. "Yeah. The sudden stop after he fell down a ravine had a lot to do with it."

"Ugh, that's a horrible way to go."

"Wouldn't be my preference. Of course, I would have kept my ass to the trail." She pointed at the cup in my hand. "Is that for me?"

"All yours," I said, passing it to her. "So where do we go from here?"

"We?" Shondra straightened to her imposing six-foot height. "Don't know about you, but I'm going home. Now that it's stopped raining, I might even be able to get my husband to mow the lawn."

"Yeah, the drizzle's been pretty steady since yesterday afternoon." I looked down at the puddle near my feet. "Seems like that could have made for a pretty wet trek for Mr. Skerrett."

"And undoubtedly had something to do with him losing his footing," Shondra said, plucking a fritter from the bakery box. "So I bet if he were still breathing, he'd be the first to admit that hike wasn't a wise decision 'cause it was a little muddy up at that scenic overlook marker. At least it gave us a pretty good shoe impression where it appears that he lost his footing."

"He didn't impress me as someone who's a fitness fanatic, so it seems kinda strange that he'd hike the trail if it was slippery."

"Charmaine, stay in this job long enough and there's no telling the amount of wacky ways you're gonna see people get themselves killed."

"I'm sure you're right," I said, thinking out loud while Shondra climbed into her car. "But it still seems strange." And beyond wacky, especially after accompanying my grandmother to Mrs. Skerrett's funeral last Saturday.

Chapter Two

"I DON'T UNDERSTAND what you're telling me," Gram said, filling her tea kettle at the sink. "Ted fell to his death because of some freak accident, or was it a suicide?"

I dropped into a chair at her kitchen table. "I don't know." Shondra had said something about Ted losing his footing, but her opinion about what happened up on that trail overlook would have to change if he had left a suicide note behind.

She heaved a sigh. "Well, what does Steve have to say about it?"

"Nothing." Plus, he had fallen asleep shortly after I arrived to make him dinner, so even if he were to get into a sharing mood, that wasn't going to happen tonight.

That's when I decided to cross the street to my grandmother's house and pick the brain of the woman who had raised me. Because after six long hours of my own company, my brain had been picked clean of everything I thought I knew about Ted Skerrett.

Gram clucked her tongue as she turned on the flame under the kettle. "That's not very helpful."

Welcome to my world.

"The sheriff's detective was still up there, working the scene, when I left, but I imagine his report will hit Shondra's inbox sometime Monday morning. Until then, I don't think anyone's going to have a lot to say about this." Not anyone with a badge, anyway.

Gram pulled two cups from the cupboard. "That won't keep people around here from talking."

I guessed that she had come to the same conclusion as I had. "Because they'll think his death has something to do with Ruth's."

Gram met my gaze, her wide eyes magnified behind her trifocals. "Char, it hasn't even been two weeks since Ruthie passed."

"I know, and I get that she'd been sick for a while, but Ted suddenly ending up at the bottom of a ravine smacks of something too weird to just be bad timing."

"Are you saying that you suspect foul play?"

"I don't know what I suspect. Has there been any gossip about him making the rounds?"

Gram shrugged. "I heard a couple of the gals at the senior center going on about Carmen having her sights set on Ted now that he was single, but I blew it off as idle speculation."

I'd witnessed my grandmother's friend, Carmen, titter like a starry-eyed teen in Ted Skerrett's presence, so this bit of news didn't surprise me in the slightest. "That's it?"

"That's all I've got," Gram said, turning her attention to the whistling kettle. "If you want real dirt, you'll have to go to Gossip Central."

In other words, back to Duke's.

Seconds later, she set two steaming cups of tea on the table and took the seat across from me.

She took a sip and stared at me over the rim of her cup. "I found myself thinking about poor Ruthie this morning, and now I can't stop thinking about Ted. The way he died really is strange, isn't it?"

I nodded.

"What are you going to do about it? Launch an investigation?"

"Me?" If we hadn't been talking about a dead guy, I would have laughed at her notion that my deputy coroner badge gave me that kind of pull. "No, but I plan on talking to someone who can."

Upon my arrival at the courthouse Monday, I made a beeline to my boss's office but stopped in my tracks when I saw County Prosecutor Frankie Rickard's door closed. Through the side window, I could see that she was on the phone.

Spotting me when she looked up, she shook her head.

Dang. I hadn't just failed to launch the death investigation I'd hoped to discuss with her; the launch pad was clearly off-limits for the time being.

"Do you need something, Charmaine?" asked Patsy Faraday, the eagle-eyed legal assistant guarding Frankie's office.

Patsy and I had shared a boss for almost a year, had eaten our way through recent divorces, and based on the highlander romance novels I'd caught her reading in the breakroom, we even shared the same favorite authors.

I guessed her to be fifteen years older than me—close to fifty, but not so much older that some sense of sisterhood through common experience couldn't be forged.

As Patsy jutted out her chin as if it were a shield, I got the message: *Move along 'cause it's never gonna happen.*

"I'll catch her later." *Preferably when you're at lunch.*

"As long as you're here..." Patsy reached behind her and handed me a short stack of manila folders. "You can file these after you make coffee."

I didn't need to witness the little curl at her lips to know that Patsy enjoyed being a senior staffer who could tell me what to do.

It didn't matter, especially when an even more senior staffer could be in receipt of a certain detective's report.

I imagined that Detective Pearson's findings could answer most of the questions that had been swirling around in my brain all weekend, so as soon as I hit the start button on the coffeemaker, I headed for Shondra's office.

But Shondra looked up from her desk and extended her arm like a traffic cop to stop me at her door. "Whatever you want, now's not a good time."

I knew she'd be in court most of the day, so now might be the only time I could get. "It'll just take a minute."

She resumed typing at the keyboard in front of her. "Talk fast."

"Has the investigating detective's report come in on

the Skerrett death?"

"Yep," Shondra said, focused on her computer monitor as I inched closer.

"And?"

"He didn't find anything to change my opinion." She blew out a sigh infused with enough irritation to tell me that there was more to this story.

"But he found something of some significance?"

Leaning back in her desk chair, she shifted her gaze to me. "Nothing that directly connects to an old dude taking a header down a ravine, no matter how loudly his sister yells in my ear about it."

I didn't know Ted had a sister. "You called her?" That made me wonder what indirect connections the detective had uncovered to warrant a follow-up phone call.

Shondra's full lips stretched into a humorless smile. "Detective Pearson gave her my name and number, probably to get her to back off while he searched the house Saturday."

"So Mr. Skerrett didn't leave a note behind or anything like that."

She shook her head. "No note, no witnesses, no nothin' other than some family drama, so his death will be recorded as an accident."

"Family drama. As in some relative making trouble for Mr. Skerrett?"

"The guy's stepchildren. Pearson talked to both of them. Didn't think there was anything to connect them to the accident, which is good enough for me." Shondra snatched up a pink phone message from her cluttered desk and unceremoniously dropped it into her wastebasket. "Unfortunately, the victim's sister wants to blame them and insists on telling me all about it."

Oh, yeah? "Want me to talk to her?" Because I'd sure like to hear what she had to say.

Shondra pursed her mouth while the phone rang at the desk outside her office. "Not much point since we don't need more information to determine manner of death."

"She's calling for you again," Shondra's administrative assistant said from the doorway.

Glaring at the blinking light on her phone, Shondra muttered an obscenity. She slanted a glance at me as she reached for the receiver. "I'll let her know you're coming."

Chapter Three

AFTER COPYING THE contents of the file on Ted Skerrett that Shondra handed me, I retreated to the recesses of the third floor, where my desk shared the dreary space with a bank of file cabinets, and started reading.

I had hoped that Detective Pearson's scene analysis would explain how Ted ended up at the bottom of that ravine.

It didn't. Instead, it read like a companion piece to Shondra's preliminary report, recording every observable aspect of the fifty-three-foot fall that resulted in Ted's broken neck and multiple contusions.

While Detective Pearson didn't offer any explanations, one line detailing the shattered cell phone found near the body suggested that Ted might have lost his footing while taking a selfie.

In the rain?

If it had been me out on that ledge, I sure wouldn't have pulled out my phone to capture the drippy moment. Instead, I would have made tracks toward the shelter of my car at the sight of the first raindrop.

Brenda Proctor, Ted's sister, had made it clear in her

statement that he was no weather weenie. He'd hit the local trails, rain or shine.

Point of pride? It sure read that way.

More interesting, Detective Pearson had indicated that she'd never seen Ted use the camera on his phone.

After taking the Gibson Lake exit off State Route 17, I slowly wound around the western shore of the tree-lined lake while my windshield wipers smeared the steady drizzle across my field of vision.

I gripped the wheel, straining to see the road that the navigation app on my phone was telling me to take. It wasn't until it repeated the instruction to make a right turn that a white brick pillar marking the entrance for Gibson Cove came into view.

Less than a minute later, I was slowing to a stop in front of what looked like undeveloped pasture land, when my phone announced the arrival at my destination.

"Really?" I peered past the rails of a weathered wood fence and saw nothing but thickets of mature fir trees bordering an overgrown field of grass.

The number on the mailbox perched on a skinny post next to a gravel driveway matched the address Brenda Proctor had provided, so I started down the drive in search of a house.

Easing around the trunk of a tall cedar, I caught a glimpse of the lake, gleaming in the same shade of gray as the gloomy sky. Between wiper swipes, fat drops splattering onto my windshield from overhead boughs trickled down like rivulets of tears.

As if I needed Mother Nature to remind me of the unfortunate reason for my visit.

Seeing Ted's new Cadillac parked in front of the detached two-car garage ahead was reminder enough. Mainly because the last time I'd seen it was at that trailhead.

I didn't recognize the older-model Toyota parked closest to the house. Assuming that it belonged to a family member who was still breathing, I pulled in behind the Caddy, climbed out of the car, and threw on my hooded raincoat.

Stepping over a water-logged dandelion patch lining the driveway, I was struck by the rustic beauty of this lakeside home. With wood siding stained in an earthy brown and clematis-covered trellises mounted between shuttered windows, it had the look of a sprawling fairy tale cottage nestled in the embrace of the trees shrouding it from the street.

A crow squawked at me from a low branch, protesting my presence. It was the only sound I heard until the front door creaked open. An older woman stepped out, appearing about as welcoming as she glared down the walkway at me. "You with the coroner's office?"

She had seemed vaguely familiar, but the second I heard the raspy quality in her voice I remembered that I had met Brenda Proctor nine days earlier at her sister-in-law's funeral.

Given all the new faces she had been introduced to that day, I didn't expect her to recognize me and reached into my tote for my badge. "Yes, ma'am. Mrs. Proctor, right?"

"Brenda," she replied in a clipped tone.

"I'm Charmaine Digby. I believe Ms. Alexander told you I'd be—"

"Yeah, yeah." She waved away my laminated badge as I joined her on the front porch. "Come in."

Taller than my five foot six by a couple of inches and broad-shouldered like her brother, Brenda led the way inside with an athletic grace.

Since she was wearing bootie-style slippers, I searched for shoes near the door to clue me in as to whether I should slip off my clogs. I saw nothing on the scuffed hardwood floor other than a couple of dust bunnies. "Should I take off my shoes?"

"Nah. Nothin' sacred about this place. On the floor, anyway."

As I followed her through a narrow hall decorated with family photos, I assumed that she meant that the value of Ted's home came from its lakefront location rather than its décor. At least that appeared to be true until we entered a spacious sitting room where rows of vintage dolls stared back at me from the shelves lining the three walls.

The Betty Boop doll displayed above a long sectional caught my eye. The flirty little red dress made her stand out from the more demure porcelain bride dolls bookending her.

I noticed that all the dolls had tags near their feet as if they had been catalogued. "Someone was a collector."

"My sister-in-law, Ruth. Rest her soul."

"Impressive." I took a seat.

Brenda didn't. Instead, the fine lines surrounding her unpainted mouth deepened as she looked down her nose at me. "Want to be impressed? Come with me."

I hadn't expected a tour but... "Okay."

Less than twenty steps down another hallway, Brenda opened the first door to the right. "Take a gander."

I stepped into a spare bedroom filled with hundreds of dolls from the last century. Stacks of boxes lined every wall with their finely dressed occupants staring out with unseeing eyes. A shelf crowded with what looked like Russian wooden dolls had been mounted above a closet with the doors removed.

When I looked inside I could see why Ruth hadn't wanted to close it off because it housed two stunning Japanese geisha dolls. "Wow."

Brenda switched on a spotlight aimed at the decorative black and gold lacquered chest supporting the geishas' matching display cases, setting the gold thread of their silk costumes aglow. "Ruth's dad worked abroad for years and used to bring her and her mom back a lot of trinkets. More treasures are squirreled away in the basement, but I always figured the best pieces were up here, where Ruth could show off her pride and joy."

"It's quite a collection. What will happen with it?"

"Ruth always hoped that her daughter would share her passion. I don't think Holly gives a hoot about a bunch of old dolls, other than what she could sell them for—and she'll get that chance soon enough."

"What do you mean?"

"She inherits the entire doll collection, so she can do what she wants with it. Same with the oil paintings that Ruth left her son. He's even more of a moneygrubber than his sister. The two of 'em came over after the funeral and started pickin' over the spoils like a couple of vultures. Not that I cared."

Yes, she did. She was so hot about it I could practically see steam coming out of her ears.

"But Ruth wanted to provide for my brother's comfort," Brenda said, wiping away a tear spilling over her sparse eyelashes. "And didn't want it to become a free-for-all. Ted appreciated that and wanted to do right by her children. That's why he had the team of appraisers come out to evaluate all this stuff."

Ted Skerrett may have appreciated the fact that his wife had designated how she wanted her family heirlooms to be dispersed, but I suspected there was a lot more to this story. "When was this?"

"Friday." Her eyes darkened a split second before she flipped off the light. "The day before they killed my brother."

"Excuse me?" I asked, bolting into the hallway to fall into step behind her. "Are you suggesting that—"

"I'm not suggesting nothin'. I'm telling you that those two had it in for Ted. It was that way from the first day they met him."

Coming to a stop in the sitting room, Brenda pulled a tissue from a pocket of her cardigan and blew her nose. "Spiteful, selfish children." She settled into a wingback chair upholstered in the same shade of burgundy as the throw pillows on the sectional and held her arms tight to her body. "Greedy ingrates, demanding their pound of flesh."

Parking myself back under Betty Boop, I pulled my notebook from my tote and started scribbling. "Pound of flesh? Could you be more specific?" And less dramatic.

Having grown up with an actress mother, I'd become

accustomed to life with a drama queen and the license to exaggerate she thought it provided her. My BS meter reached its tipping point with my mom when she couldn't make it home for my sixteenth birthday because she had to work ... with a chakra therapist in Sedona. It became crystal clear to me then that people would say whatever they thought they could get away with.

Much like my mother, it seemed that Brenda believed she had honed that skill to perfection.

Leaning back, I smiled politely. *Think again.*

Brenda sharpened her gaze, her cheeks flushed. "Do I have to spell it out for you?"

I wished she would, because it would make writing my report so much easier. "Just tell me what happened Friday."

She vented a breath. "Holly and Marc arrived at the house just as the appraisers were leaving and started making all sorts of ugly accusations."

"Like what?"

"Saying that Ted was trying to cheat them out of their inheritance."

Which might be the conclusion I'd jump to if I saw my stepfather chatting with an appraiser.

"Ridiculous," Brenda said with a dismissive wave of her hand. "And frankly insulting to poor Teddy."

She made a point of blotting her dry eyes, which only added to my suspicion that Teddy had been making sure he wouldn't come out on the poor end of this deal.

"Because having the appraisers on-site was for the purpose of..."

"Fairness, of course."

Nope. There was definitely something more to it than that. "Uh-huh."

"Given the terms of Ruth's will, and how those kids disappeared from her life the last few years, Ted's efforts were more than generous."

I doubted that Marc and Holly would agree with her. "Were any threats made?"

Brenda studied her slippers. "Not in so many words, but Marc was spittin' mad, sayin' he was going to get a lawyer."

"To contest the will?"

"I guess. Won't change nothin', though. The money the pissant wants is already gone."

Money? I thought we were talking about the contents of the house that had been appraised. "What do you mean?"

"His mother spent money like it was water. Buzzed through most of her savings after she got the cancer diagnosis last year." A wisp of a satisfied smile curled Brenda's lips. "We sure had fun, though."

We? "What'd you do?"

"A world cruise, a month in Tahiti, Broadway shows, skydiving—pretty much everything you could put on a bucket list, Ted and Ruth did."

"You said 'we,' so you got to tag along on these trips?" And help Ruth spend her money.

"As Ruth's caregiver. Plus, she was a generous friend."

Maybe. But something about Brenda hanging around here by herself felt off. "Just the three of you sharing these big adventures?"

"Just us." Brenda turned up the wattage of her thin-lipped smile. "The three amigos."

I didn't know Marc and Holly beyond our brief exchange at their mother's funeral, but I couldn't help but be sympathetic considering the frustrating situation their mom had bequeathed to them. But would it have motivated one of them to do any real physical harm to Ted? Brenda certainly thought so, but I hadn't heard anything that I could take to Shondra that she wouldn't chalk up to family drama.

After Brenda provided me with the name of the Port Townsend appraisers Ted had used, I scanned my notes to see if I needed any other details for my report.

"You mentioned that Marc and Holly arrived close to the time that the appraisers were leaving. When exactly was that?"

"I was making dinner, so it would have been around four-thirty." Brenda pursed her lips. "I remember because I had to turn off the stove to find out what all the commotion was about."

"And when did Ted leave for the trail?"

"Close to five."

"Last thing for the timeline, are you aware of when Marc and Holly left?"

Brenda shot me a frown of annoyance. "It was within seconds of Ted."

"So you think they followed him to the trail?"

"I *know* they did."

"How do you know?"

"I just know. The same way I knew that something was very wrong with Ted."

Holding Brenda's gaze, I almost felt like her brother was looking back at me. And it wasn't just the deep set of her dark eyes. It was the angular cheeks and the little dimple in her chin identical to Ted's.

Holy crap! They were twins. Obviously fraternal, but that would explain why she was so quick to call the police Friday night. "So you 'sensed' that your brother was in trouble?"

"That twin spidey-sense stuff?"

I nodded.

She blotted her eyes, this time for real. "He was the intuitive one, not me. I just knew that something was wrong when Teddy didn't make it back in time for dinner. He just wasn't one to miss a meal."

With everything she'd told me this morning, I didn't doubt that for a minute.

"What about the cell phone the police found near Ted?"

She glowered. "What about it?"

"You mentioned in your statement that you didn't think Ted would have been using it to take a picture."

"He was serious about his training. Trust me, he wouldn't have stopped to take a picture."

Ordinarily, I discount anything that follows the words "Trust me." Not this time. Brenda had told the absolute truth.

"Training for what?" I asked.

"A 10K marathon next month. He didn't want me to show him up like I did a couple years back, so he'd been training hard, hitting that trail every day."

"Just the Spirit Rim trail? It was my understanding that Ted liked to hike some of the other local trails."

"He did. But he didn't just hike Spirit Rim; he'd run."

"Every day."

"Pretty much. Up to the crest and back."

Which could have made Ted easy pickings for anyone familiar with his exercise routine.

"Did you ever run with him on that trail?"

Brenda nodded. "Obviously not often enough."

"Would you say your brother was pretty sure-footed?"

"He wouldn't go sliding off the dang trail, if that's what you're asking."

That's exactly what I was asking.

"He was pushed." She narrowed her gaze to a piercing squint. "Now what I want to know is what you're gonna do about it."

If I'd learned anything from the handful of death investigations I'd flown solo on, it was to avoid promising anything that I couldn't personally deliver. "That's a determination that Ms. Alexander will make."

"I'm no fool. I know how this looks to all of you, but I'm telling you—Ted didn't just fall off that ledge."

I had no doubt she believed that. Heck, I was even beginning to have my own suspicions, but I wasn't the one who needed to be convinced. "I'll make sure that your feelings are made clear in my report."

I dropped my notebook into my tote to signal the end of this interview and pushed off the sectional.

"I also need you to do something for me," Brenda said, rising to her feet. "Actually, for Ted."

I didn't like the direction this was going. "I will if I can."

She pulled a folded sheet of paper from her pocket and handed it to me. "Talk to Ruth's kids before you hand in that report."

As I glanced down at the two addresses she'd listed, Brenda pointed at the bottom of the page. "I also included my contact information in case you needed it."

Just like on the statement she'd provided Detective Pearson, Brenda had used Ted's address instead of her permanent residence. "How long do you plan on staying in the area?"

"Too soon to say. I can tell you this, though—I'm not planning on selling right away."

Selling? "You own this house?"

"Never expected that he'd be leaving it to me, but it stands to reason. I'm all the family Ted had."

Obviously, Ruth's children didn't count in the Skerrett family dynamic.

Brenda tapped the paper in my hand. "So, will you promise me that you'll talk to them?"

"You can count on it."

Chapter Four

ALMOST AN HOUR later, I was stepping onto the third-floor landing of the courthouse when three women with juror badges passed me on their way downstairs.

Since it was too early for the typical lunch recess, and Shondra was walking out of Judge Navarro's courtroom looking like she wanted to grind someone under the heel of her black pumps, no one had to tell me that something had gone wrong.

I was no dummy. I knew this wasn't the optimum time to strike up a conversation. But she was closing fast and had just made eye contact, so I figured that was as much of an invitation to approach as I was going to get today.

"That chat with Brenda Proctor turned out to be more interesting than I thought it would be," I said, falling into step with Shondra.

She slanted me a glance. "Do I have the appearance of someone who wants to hear this right now?"

"No, but I thought you should know that there's a possibility that Detective Pearson didn't get the whole story when he spoke to the other family members."

Shondra stopped so abruptly at the door to the prosecutor's office that I had to hit the brakes not to run into her. "I have a missing witness that I need to produce in the next three hours, so if there's a point to this story, I suggest you hurry up and make it."

"I'd like to get their statements."

"Go ahead." Resting her hand on the brass door knob, she sharpened her gaze. "But don't give anyone the impression that we're opening an investigation, 'cause we're not."

"Yes, ma'am." Message received loud and clear.

"And don't mention this to Detective Pearson." Shondra swung the door open. "I don't need any more aggravation today."

"Got it," I said, following her past the desk of a wary-looking receptionist.

"Is someone having a bad day?" she whispered before Shondra was out of earshot.

I didn't need any aggravation either, especially from one of the senior staffers who could get me fired, so I nodded like a mute and scurried toward the bowels of the administrative wing. I had two interviews to schedule.

When I called Marc Worley, he seemed eager to talk and suggested that we meet at five o'clock at Mama's Kitchen, near where he worked as an insurance sales agent in Everett. His sister Holly didn't return my calls, but he had told me she was hard to reach during the day, so I made a mental note to try her again after my meeting with him.

I knew how bad the commuter traffic could be on the

five-lane stretch of interstate north of Seattle, so I drove over to Kingston and caught the three-ten ferry to allow for sitting for an hour on a freeway. Good thing too, because I pulled into the Mama's Kitchen parking lot with only a minute to spare.

Much like Duke's with its afternoon-pie happy hour, I saw a sign by the door indicating that Mama's featured an early bird special. That explained why most of the tables were occupied by seniors.

What I didn't see was a man in his late forties sitting by himself. But when I told the gum-chewing hostess that I was meeting someone, she led me past several elderly couples chowing down on the meatloaf special to a corner table. There I found the portly man I had met last month at his mother's funeral.

Marc scooted back his wooden chair and stood, revealing a wrinkled Oxford shirt straining at the buttons. "Charmaine?"

I took no offense that he didn't remember me, and extended my hand. "Hi, Marc. Thanks for meeting with me so quickly."

After waving off the menu from the hostess, who took the hint to leave us alone, I turned to the wiry brunette who had been sitting across the table from him and was surprised to see his sister. "Hello, Holly."

With her long, angular face and sinewy arms, Holly Worley Hines had reminded me of a greyhound when I first saw her at her mom's service. Sleek and graceful as she negotiated the crowd, unlike her balding bulldog of a brother.

Holly offered me a tepid smile. "Hope you don't mind me barging in. Marc told me you were meeting."

I wondered what else they had talked about as I shook her cool, paper-dry hand. "Of course not."

She slid over one chair and gestured for me to take the seat she had just vacated. If I wanted to have a prayer of reading their body language with any accuracy, I needed them to both sit across from me.

"I wonder if I could trade you seats," I said to Marc before he settled back down. "I'm one of those note-takers who needs to spread out and I don't want to crowd anyone."

"No problem." He dropped into the chair next to Holly with a little wheeze, as if the three seconds of exertion had exhausted him, and exchanged glances of annoyance with his sister.

I didn't make a lot out of it. They shared at least forty-five years of family history—plenty of time to get on one another's nerves under the best of life's circumstances.

And we all knew that we hadn't gathered together to chat about anything fun.

I pasted a friendly smile on my face. "I don't know how much your brother told you," I said to Holly while I pulled a pen and notebook from my tote bag. "But since you both spoke to Ted Skerrett shortly before his death, the county coroner has a few questions."

Well, she didn't, really, but I did.

Holly gave me an impatient nod. "Fine."

Venting another wheezy breath, Marc leaned back while a waitress in her early twenties placed a dinner salad oozing with creamy dressing in front of him.

"You sure I can't get you anything?" she asked Holly.

Holly glared at her brother's salad like she wanted to

dump it over his head. "No, thank you."

The waitress took a step back as if to get out of the line of fire and gave me a nervous smile. "How about you?"

My growling stomach wanted a big slab of that meatloaf, but I'd come here to satisfy a need for information, not food. So I ordered an unsweetened iced tea and hoped that the noise of the room would drown out the rumbling of my empty tummy.

"Hope you don't mind if I dig in. I'm starving," Marc said to me, fork in hand.

I would have preferred that he not obscure the lower portion of his face with a fork or napkin, but I didn't want to say anything to cause the level of tension at the table to spike. "Go ahead."

While he forked a drippy bite of iceberg lettuce into his mouth, I focused my attention on Holly. "I'd like to start with your relationship with Mr. Skerrett over the last year. How would you describe it?"

Narrowing her eyes, Holly waited for the girl delivering my tea to leave before answering. "Civil, at least until our mother passed away."

Marc shook his head and muttered something unintelligible.

"Care to elaborate?" I asked, trying to ignore the blue cheese dressing smears around his mouth.

He pointed at me with his fork. "What part of 'He was a self-serving jerk' didn't you understand?"

Since his messy mouth had been full, none of it.

I took a sip of tea and dabbed my lips with my napkin to clue him in to do the same. "You're characterizing Ted Skerrett as being self-serving how, exactly?"

"He lived off my mother like a leech for over twenty years." Marc's lips stretched into a sneer of contempt. "And bled her dry."

"Him and his sister," Holly added while Marc went back to work on his salad. "The two of them were in it together at the end."

This sounded a lot more conspiratorial than what I was expecting to hear. "Did your mother ever express any concern about Ted or Brenda?"

Holly sighed. "Of course not. Mom was the queen of avoidance. Unfortunately, that was something that only got worse after her diagnosis. And with Ted managing all of the finances by then, she was kept blissfully unaware of how bad things were."

"He wouldn't even let us have a minute alone with her," Marc added between bites. "He would always claim that he didn't want our mom to get upset, but ol' Ted just didn't want her to hear the truth."

"I can imagine how frustrating that was for you." It ran counter to Brenda's story, but since she was one of the "amigos" who had been helping Ruth spend her money, I found Marc and Holly's depiction of Ted to be more credible.

Marc nodded. "It's tough when you have a mother who won't listen to reason."

Yeah. I could vouch for that.

It was also tough to not stare at the guy across from you when a tiny sliver of carrot had attached itself to the goo at the corner of his mouth.

Holly heaved another sigh. "And thinks we simply can't accept her being with another man. Like we were begrudging her finding someone. The only thing I couldn't accept was that she was with *that* man!"

Smacking his lips while he chewed, Marc turned to his sister. "Exactly."

She scowled at him. "Will you wipe your mouth, please? You're disgusting."

Sheepishly, he ran his napkin over the fleshy contours of his five-o'clock shadow and then pushed away his empty salad bowl. "What are you gonna do?"

I wasn't sure if he was referencing his eating habits or his mother's taste in men, but I knew I needed to glean as many pertinent details as I could before the next course arrived.

That required getting them thinking about the scene the day of Ted's death. "I understand that Ted had arranged for some appraisers to come out to the house on Friday."

Holly's brown eyes narrowed to a squint. "Yes, he acted all magnanimous, like he was doing Marc a favor by letting him know how much he could get if he let Ted sell one of the paintings Mom had bequeathed to him."

"That's when I knew we had to get over there before he started selling off the estate without our permission," Marc said with a determined set to his jaw as he exchanged glances with his sister.

"Marc called me and we got on the next ferry." She directed her gaze at me. "Just to claim what was rightfully ours. Because despite what our mother's will says, she never intended to leave Ted everything."

According to Brenda, that was exactly what Ruth had intended, but I saw no indication of deception in the siblings sitting across from me. Instead, what I assumed had been a long-simmering stew of angry emotions bubbled at the surface, lending credence to their tag-team account.

"Then what happened?" I asked, my pen poised over my notebook.

"We got to the house just as the appraisers were leaving. I tried to talk to them before they got into their car—make them understand that Ted didn't have the right to speak for us." Holly leaned in, curling her hands into white-knuckled fists. "That's when Daddy dearest came running out of the house to deny me even that."

That sure didn't sound like the easygoing Ted Skerrett I'd known. "But they had to have realized that there are things in the house that are yours, like all those dolls."

Holly rolled her eyes. "All those stupid dolls. I certainly never asked for them, but I should at least be able to go in and haul them out of there, along with anything else that my mother promised me. Marc should have that right, too."

I locked gazes with him. "Promised you in her will?"

"There's stuff that Mom knew was important to us—that we should keep in the family," Marc said, looking with sudden interest at his salad bowl.

I assumed that was because he had chosen to avoid answering my question. "And that's specifically stated in her will?"

The hiss of air escaping Marc's lips answered for him.

"Not specifically," Holly admitted with icy resignation. "But it was what we'd talk about almost every time we saw her in the last year."

Marc nodded. "Yeah, that she was willing to talk

about because she wanted us all to be prepared. Even
had Hol and me put our names on the family stuff that
we wanted."

"She used to joke from her hospital bed that this was
her way of getting us to help her clean out her basement." Holly pressed a napkin to her watery eyes. "I
guess Ted decided to play this so that the joke really was
on us."

This certainly didn't fit Brenda's description of selfish
children who never visited their mother, nor had I heard
anything to support her claim that they had anything to
do with Ted's death. "Going back to when Mr. Skerrett
came out of the house, what happened after the
appraisers left?"

"Nothing," the siblings said in what sounded like
well-rehearsed unison.

I didn't need to be able to observe the tension in
their body language to know they were lying. "You want
me to believe that no other words were exchanged?"

Holly aimed an angry glare at me. "Nothing of any
significance, no matter what that witch in our mother's
house may have told you."

"So you just accepted the situation, said your good-
byes, and left."

"Since Ted said he was going to call the cops, he
didn't leave us a lot of choice."

"Plus, we had a ferry to catch," Marc was quick to
add.

Too quickly, because he had forgotten one important
little detail. "You had just gotten there."

"There wasn't any point in sticking around. Ted was
leaving, and if we didn't do the same he said that Brenda

wouldn't hesitate to call the cops."

And I thought the relationship with my soon-to-be stepfather was complicated.

"Speaking of cops, Marc, you said in your statement to Detective Pearson that you followed Mr. Skerrett from the house to the Spirit Rim trailhead."

Marc's face blanched under a sheen of sweat. "Uh…"

His sister turned her glare on him. "I'm sure you didn't use those *exact* words."

"Uh… maybe."

Now, she was the one hissing like a deflating balloon.

"We only wanted to talk to him," Marc muttered as if he were pleading his case to a jury.

"And did you?"

"I … uh … no. He ran up the trail before I had a chance."

"Did you follow him up the trail?" I asked, watching him carefully.

He peered into his salad bowl as if he wanted to disappear under one of the remaining lettuce leaves while Holly snickered.

"Seriously?" she asked. "He got winded walking to this table."

Marc grimaced. "Thanks a lot."

Okay, no shocker that Marc wouldn't stray far from his car.

I fixed my gaze on the greyhound. "How about you?"

She gave me a withering look of contempt. "And ruin a three-hundred-dollar pair of heels?"

There was something about her haughty non-answer that didn't feel right, aside from the fact that Holly had just channeled my mother. "So you didn't talk to Ted before he headed up the trail."

"I tried." She shook her head. "As usual, it was a complete waste of time."

So far the siblings hadn't given me much beyond a good reason why they wouldn't be shedding any tears at Ted's funeral. "Did you see anyone else coming or going on the trail?"

I got more head-shaking.

"Any cars parked there other than Ted's?"

"A couple," Holly said. "I didn't pay much attention to them. I was a little...preoccupied."

Marc shot her a dismissive glance. "Yeah. Bitching at me like this is all my fault."

Seething, she folded her arms tight across her chest. "Well, it's certainly not mine."

Spending ten minutes with these two made me glad I was an only child.

"Do you agree?" I asked Marc. "There were two other cars there?"

"The one I parked next to was a red Jeep. Couldn't tell you about the other one. Someone was *distracting* me at the time."

Injecting enough steel into her jaw to snap her brother's head off, Holly shifted her gaze to me. "Are we done here?"

I sure wanted to be. "Unless there's anything else that you saw before you left that night."

Marc sucked in a breath a nanosecond before the waitress swooped in to collect his salad bowl. "You think this wasn't an accident. That's why you're asking all these questions."

I forced a smile. "We'd just like to talk to anyone who

saw Mr. Skerrett on that trail."

And given the likelihood that I'd be able to track down the drivers of those two cars, good luck with that.

Chapter Five

"WHAT'S THIS?" STEVE asked, following me and Fozzie into his living room.

I didn't understand his indignant tone, as if I'd breached some sort of protocol. "Since when do you have a problem with me bringing Fozzie over?"

"I don't." Steve looked past the black chow mix sniffing the takeout bag in my hand and pointed at the grease-stained sack. "Is that on your diet?"

I settled into the middle cushion of his chocolate brown leather sectional and tossed him the bag. "Don't be the food police, and I'll have you know that I bought those fries for you." Minus the few I treated myself to after I wolfed down an overcooked chicken burger.

"Yeah?" Fozzie danced at Steve's feet while he reached into the bag. "They're cold."

"Well, they were hot when I bought them an hour ago."

He frowned at the burger joint's orange logo emblazoned on the bag. "In Kingston? What were you doing there?"

"I had to go to Everett to interview someone," I said to his backside while Fozzie followed him into the kitchen.

"Really. I didn't think you guys had any open coroner cases."

"We don't. I just needed to corroborate someone's story."

Steve stood in front of his microwave oven with a suspicious glint in his eye. "Whose story would that be?"

I turned to face the TV to let him know that I wasn't in the mood for an interrogation. "No one you know. Can we change the subject now?"

"Why don't you want to tell me about this?"

Because I didn't want to hear another lecture about getting overly involved in someone else's investigation.

While I wrestled to come up with a good evasive answer, the microwave dinged and I bounded to my feet. "Maybe I should put Fozzie in the car. He'll never let you eat those fries in peace otherwise."

"I have a better solution," Steve said, opening the glass slider to his fenced backyard.

The second Fozzie bolted out the door, Steve directed his attention to me. "You were saying?"

I sunk back down in the leather cushions and hugged my arms to my chest. "I don't know why you're making a big deal about this. There's not that much else to say."

Taking the seat next to me, he popped a steaming golden fry into his mouth. "Sure."

I stole a fry from his plate and pointed it at him. "Not that it's any of your business, but I was following up on a lead for Shondra."

Steve's mouth curled into a lopsided grin. "A lead, huh?"

"Yes, smartass. When someone accuses a family

member of murder, I call that a lead worth pursuing."

Steve's grin disappeared. "Exactly who are you talking about?"

"Ted Skerrett's sister."

"The one who reported him missing."

"She doesn't think his fall was an accident," I said, chewing.

Steve set the plate of fries on the coffee table. "Yeah, Pearson mentioned that there had been some sort of argument earlier in the day."

"I spoke with everyone involved."

"Of course you did."

"Hey, it's my job to follow up so that the person signing the death certificate has the full story."

Steve reached for my hand and linked his fingers with mine. "So, does she have the full story now?"

"She will as soon as I write up the report."

"Then this non-case of yours should be closed."

"Yep, this should be a done deal." Brenda wouldn't be happy to hear about it, but hopefully that would be Shondra's problem, not mine.

"Good." Leaning back, Steve's dark brown eyes gleamed with carnal intent as he pulled me on top of him. "Because there's another matter I'd like to discuss."

Settling into his warmth, I tasted his salty lips. "And what matter would that be?"

He answered with a kiss, long and deep.

"What's that?" I asked when I came up for air. "I can barely hear you."

Steve pulled off my T-shirt in one smooth move and proceeded to lavish my neck with kisses. Working his way up, he whispered, "Can you hear me now?"

Oh, yes. "Loud and clear."

✳

"Okay," Shondra said, looking up from the three-page report she had been reading while eating her lunch at her desk. "With no witnesses to support Ms. Proctor's claims, we are done with this inquiry."

I had spent the morning expecting to hear as much. But ever since I had submitted my summary of the family members' statements, I couldn't shake the nagging feeling that Brenda could be right.

Ted didn't just fall off that ledge.

After wiping her hands on a napkin, Shondra scribbled her initials below my signature on the last page, tucked the report into Ted Skerrett's file, and handed it to me. "Give that to Frankie."

"Yes, ma'am." I fingered the skinny file folder. Too skinny, considering everything I'd learned about Ted Skerrett in the last forty-eight hours.

With her sandwich an inch from her mouth, Shondra's ebony eyes cut to me. "I don't see you moving."

"Sorry. I was just thinking that the timing of Mr. Skerrett's death was...well...weird."

"I'm sure it's not the time he would've picked."

I started for the door. "Yeah, I'm sure." But that didn't make his tumble down that ravine any less weird.

"Charmaine?"

With one foot in the hallway, I looked back.

"You completed your report, and there was nothing in it to suggest that we should spend one more minute on this. Now let this go."

"Right," I said, heading toward Frankie's office with a tight grip on Ted's file.

I needed to get out of the office and clear my head. I also needed to fill my growling stomach with some food—preferably free food. So, taking advantage of the break from the rain, I changed into the sneakers that I keep at my desk, grabbed my tote, and set off down the hill.

Not that I made a habit out of checking up on Steve, but when I approached the crosswalk at Third Street, I couldn't help but notice that his unmarked cruiser was parked in front of the police station.

Nothing would have improved my mood faster than to continue our "conversation" from last night, so I texted him an invitation to join me.

Since my phone buzzed with his reply before I made it to Duke's front door, I smiled with the same flutter of hope I had twenty years earlier when I thought Steve was crossing the school gymnasium to ask me to dance.

Nope. His soon-to-be steady girlfriend, Heather Beckett, was standing right behind me, and she was the one who held him in her arms for most of the next three years.

Not that I cared. Much.

At least now I felt assured that I was the object of Steve's affection. And as long as I didn't overanalyze every little bump we'd encountered since venturing past the boundaries of the friend zone back in August, maybe I could keep feeling that way.

Of course, his terse reply of *Can't* effectively threw a bucket of ice water on that flutter, dousing my hope that my lips would touch anything the least bit fun over the next half hour.

"Stupid diet," I muttered, resenting the mouth-watering aroma of bacon cheeseburgers assailing me as I stepped inside the crowded diner.

It didn't stop my nose from leading me to the source of all that artery-clogging grease: the grill, where my curmudgeon of a great-uncle was sautéing onions for a patty melt. "Hey," I said to him.

Glaring through the window over the grill, Duke answered with one of the more colorful strings of obscenities he'd picked up during his twenty years in the Navy.

I tracked the scowl he was aiming at a corner table, where Lucille was sitting with two members of the Gray Ladies, an early morning exercise group named for the matching heather gray sweats they wore to the senior center up the street. "They're here late."

He turned that scowl on me. "More like they've over-stayed their welcome."

"Have they been here all morning?"

Instead of responding, Duke assembled the patty melt, dumped a basket of fries next to it, and slid the plate onto the shiny aluminum counter in front of him. "Order up," he barked, his glare fixed on Lucille.

She held up a finger like she needed a minute.

"That's it," he announced with enough volume for ninety-one-year-old Stanley, one of the regulars at the counter, to look up over his newspaper as if a more entertaining story was about to break. "It's time for the wake they're holding for Ted to wrap up."

"Wake?" Where the ladies could be swapping stories about the guy?

And Duke wanted to shoo them away the second I got here? "Not so fast."

He glowered at me. "Excuse me?"

Needing to run some quick interference, I pointed at the collection of order tickets hanging from the aluminum wheel above the grill. "You have customers to feed. Let me handle this."

Growling like a caged lion, he reached for an order ticket. "If Luce doesn't get back to work in the next five seconds—"

"I said I'll handle it." I smiled sweetly at him as I picked up the patty melt for delivery. "Where?"

Duke gave a nod toward the counter. "Guy next to Stan."

After doing my waitressly duty, I topped off all the coffee cups at the counter to buy myself a little time with Lucille and the ladies.

"More decaf, Stan?" I asked.

He lowered his newspaper. "Yup, I'm out."

"Sorry." I reached behind me for the orange-handled carafe. "I'm sure Lucille didn't mean to neglect you."

"She's been a little preoccupied." He leaned close while I poured, the glimmer in his eyes magnified by his horn-rimmed glasses. "I think something big is going down in the corner."

"Oh yeah? Maybe I should see if anyone needs anything." I gave him a wink, grabbed the fresh pot of regular, and headed for the corner table.

"Afternoon, ladies," I said, meeting Lucille's gaze

while I filled her cup.

She motioned toward the seventy-somethings, sitting solemnly around the table. "Char, you remember Winnie and Nadine."

"Of course." In the months since coming home after my divorce, I'd served Winnie Dearborn and Nadine Grunfeld gallons of rotgut coffee after their exercise class. But never before had one of them burst into tears while I did it.

"I'm so sorry," Winnie mumbled as she pushed her wireframes to the crown of her soft graying curls and pressed a crumpled napkin to her eyes.

Nadine patted her on the shoulder. "Honey, you have nothing to be sorry for."

"Actually, I'm the one who's sorry. I'm intruding." I shot Lucille a sideways glance. *Or am I?*

She pulled out the chair next to her. "Winnie was one of the last people to see Ted before he disappeared."

Then that made her someone I needed to talk to before she disappeared from the cafe.

Setting the two carafes on the table, I took the seat Lucille had offered. "Where did you see him?" *On the trail?*

"At Schmidt's." Winnie wiped away another tear. "We had a ..." Pressing her lips together, she stared into the inky depths of her cup. "We met for lunch."

Since I knew her to have been a close friend of Ted's late wife, I wasn't the least bit suspicious about Winnie meeting him at a waterfront sandwich shop. What grabbed my attention was the fact that she had censored herself.

Why? Because she didn't want to admit that it had

been more than a friendly lunch?

"Speaking of lunch," Nadine said, pushing away from the table. "I promised my daughter that I'd babysit so that she could get out of the house for a couple of hours." She flashed me a smile that didn't reach her eyes. "Grandma's making their favorite mac n' cheese, and I'm late. Nice seeing you again."

Nadine might make some mighty fine cheesy macaroni, but that had nothing to do with why she was leaving.

Ordinarily, I'm not one to make a big deal out of someone bending the truth to get out of an awkward situation. But since we had just been talking about a guy who died under some very strange circumstances, this wasn't one of those times.

Nadine leaned over to give Winnie a warm hug. "Take care. Call if you want to talk."

Winnie nodded. "Thanks for staying."

"Of course. What are friends for?"

After the little bell above the door signaled Nadine's departure, Winnie took a sip of coffee and then reached for her purse. "I should get going too. I'm sure someone's waiting for the table."

I glanced over at the curmudgeon with the silver crew cut standing behind the grill, and he gave me a *hurry it up* look. "I wonder if I could ask you a question before you go."

Sitting very still, she blinked. "What kind of question?"

"You know that I work for Frankie as a deputy coroner."

Her blue-eyed gaze tightened. "Yes."

"We're still trying to piece together what happened to cause Mr. Skerrett's fall." Okay, since I had just completed the only inquiry my department was going to make into this matter, that statement was a stretch. But Winnie Dearborn didn't know that.

"I don't think that I can help you with that," she said with a calm that belied the white-knuckled grip she had on the table.

Clearly, she knew more than she wanted to admit. "How was Mr. Skerrett's mood during lunch?"

Winnie's eyes flooded with tears, spilling over onto her plump cheeks. "It had been just fine."

Had? "Did something happen to change it?"

She choked back a sob. "I had to break up with him."

Chapter Six

THE SECOND THE door jingled shut behind Winnie, I pulled Lucille into the kitchen. "She broke up with him?! Did you know they were seeing one another?"

Lucille shook her head, the points of her platinum bob framing the satisfaction dancing at her lips. "Found out a couple of hours before you did. Overheard her and Nadine talking. Not that I was eavesdropping, of course."

"Of course not." And I wasn't about to criticize the Queen of Gossip Central for what she did best, especially when I wanted to find out what else she'd heard.

"Hey," Duke groused as we passed by. "Are we going to do some actual work sometime today?"

I waved him away. "I'm giving her my lunch order."

"You know you could sit out front and do that like a normal paying customer," he called after me.

"I could, but I wouldn't want to shock your system."

"Shock whose system?" my great-aunt Alice asked, glancing up from the German chocolate cake she was decorating.

"Never mind." Pulling Duke's desk chair to Alice's butcher block worktable in the center of the kitchen, I pointed for Lucille to sit. "Does she know?"

"Know what?" Alice aimed her pastry bag at me as if it were loaded with something deadlier than chocolate buttercream. "What the heck is going on?"

"Lucille and I just heard something very interesting," I said, planting my butt on the wooden stool next to her.

Her hazel eyes wide behind wire-rimmed trifocals, Alice set her pastry bag to the side. "Something juicy?"

Lucille leaned in. "You saw Winnie and several of the Gray Ladies here for their usual after-class breakfast, right?"

Alice nodded. "Looked like a good turnout."

"Well, after most of 'em left around nine, Winnie and Nadine stayed on, guzzling coffee in that corner for hours."

Alice knit her brows. "It's not bad enough that Stanley hangs out here all day to drink his fill of decaf? Now the Gray Ladies are gonna start sucking us dry?"

Sheesh. It wasn't the first time I'd heard the fiery former redhead mimic her skinflint husband of over fifty years. But since we all knew that I was the primary offender when it came to treating their diner like an all-I-could-drink coffee bar, I wanted to move this debrief along.

"Trust me, they weren't here for a caffeine fix." I motioned to Lucille. "Fast forward to the part about Ted."

Alice blinked. "Ted Skerrett?"

"It seems that Winnie and Ted were an item," Lucille whispered conspiratorially.

Alice's jaw dropped. "Ruth only died two weeks ago!"

"I know." Contempt tugged at the corners of Lucille's

coral-painted lips. "He didn't waste any time."

"So neither one of you had known anything about them getting together?" I asked.

They shook their heads.

Since it was next to impossible for any he-ing and she-ing to go on amongst the local seniors without it becoming gossip circuit breaking news, I found this very curious.

"What else did Winnie have to say?" I asked Lucille.

She shrugged. "Not much at first. In fact, she got super-quiet when the girls started gabbing about how hard Carmen was taking Ted's death."

"Carmen!" Alice slapped the table, sending up a puff of flour dust. "Was that old fool trying to nab herself another husband?"

Lucille rolled her eyes. "He was newly single and breathing. What do you think?"

Well, he wasn't breathing now. I couldn't imagine Carmen had anything to do with that outcome, but since she might have seen Ted last Friday, I made a mental note to speak with her. Winnie, too.

"Back to Winnie," I said to Lucille. "Did she tell you how long she and Ted had been an item?"

"Not in so many words, and not until it was just her and Nadine at the table, and they ran out of napkins."

Alice scowled. "How could they run out? I filled all the holders before yesterday's pie happy hour."

"Two hours of Winnie cryin' over Ted," Lucille retorted. "That's how. Anyway, when Nadine called me over for more napkins, I realized that I'd better help console poor Winnie before all her carrying on upset the other customers."

"Sure." We all knew this was more about first-hand dirt than consolation, but I wasn't about to call Lucille's bluff.

"And when I say 'carrying on,' let me tell you Winnie was in love with that man."

Alice slapped the table again. "Really!"

Lucille nodded. "Seemed like he'd really swept her off her feet over the last couple of weeks."

"You don't think they were ..." Alice pumped her fist in an unmistakably sexual way.

Something else I figured she'd picked up from her sailor husband. "Aunt Alice!"

"What? We're all adults here." She pierced Lucille with the intensity of her gaze. "Well? Were they or weren't they?"

Lucille shook her head. "I don't think so, but it was pretty dang clear that they'd been talking about getting married."

"Holy smokes," Alice said. "And no one else knew about this until this morning?"

"No, Nadine surely knew."

"Why do you say it that way?" I asked Lucille.

Her thin lips drew into a sad smile. "The best friend always knows. Besides, I could tell by the way Nadine was talking. She wasn't hearing about this thing with Ted for the first time."

"How about Winnie breaking it off with him? Did she know about that?" Because Nadine made herself scarce before the subject arose in my presence.

"Trust me." Lucille pointed an index finger at me. "That was news to just you and me."

"An almost engagement, a breakup, and then Ted's

found the next day." Alice stared blankly at the industrial oven warming my backside. "I swear. I might need a score card to keep up with everything that's been going on since Ruthie's funeral."

"I know," Lucille said. "That's why I didn't want to leave the table once Winnie started to spill. I didn't wanna miss anything."

But I still felt like I was missing something. "I appreciate that Winnie must feel like she's been on an emotional roller coaster, but what do you think she meant about *having* to break up with Ted?"

Lucille shrugged. "She sorta tiptoed around it, but you could tell she was feeling guilty about rushing into something with the husband of one of her best friends."

Alice nodded. "Of course she did. It was too soon. Anyone, including Carmen, would know that. Although I'm sure he was his usual charming self with those girls. He certainly acted that way at the funeral."

Yes, he had. At the time I had assumed that Ted was skilled at compartmentalizing his emotions. Now it seemed as if he had embarked upon a recruiting mission for the next Mrs. Skerrett.

✻

"So you don't think that it's strange that Winnie Dearborn and Ted Skerrett were talking about getting married?" I asked Steve while he watched me chop lettuce for the taco salad I was making for our dinner.

He blew out a breath. "You obviously do."

"Well, yeah. His wife had only been dead two weeks."

"You're right. He should've waited at least three

weeks."

I stopped chopping. "This isn't funny."

"Didn't say it was. It's just that he wouldn't have been the first person around here to rush into marriage."

I knew Steve was referring to my impulsive mother announcing her engagement to our former biology teacher before the ink on her latest divorce papers was dry.

Not a subject I wanted to revisit tonight—not when Winnie's revelation about her relationship with Ted Skerrett had my brain cells on overload.

"It still seems strange, though," I said. "Winnie calls everything off, he goes home and gets into a beef over Ruth's estate, and then falls to his death a couple hours later."

Steve didn't respond so I locked gazes with him. "Seriously. You don't find this even a little bit suspicious?"

He lifted the bottle of mineral water he'd found in my refrigerator in mock salute. "Not something I see every day, I'll give you that."

"I rest my case."

"Chow Mein, I'd like to trust that you mean that."

Despite softening his remark by using the nickname he'd bestowed on me back in the third grade, the hard set to Steve's jaw told me that I'd just been warned.

"Then maybe you should," I said, turning my attention to the pan of beef and onions simmering on the stove.

"I would if you'd stop trying to play detective."

"I resent that. I've simply been doing my job."

"Yeah, that's what you said last night."

"And it's still true."

Steve leaned against the counter. "And that report you were talking about. Did you give it to Shondra?"

I focused on a translucent bit of onion I was pushing around with a wooden spoon to avoid making eye contact. "Yep."

"What'd she say about it?"

"That we were done with our inquiry."

"Then that's that, right?"

"The death certificate has been signed, so yes."

He drained the bottle and set it down with more force than necessary. "That's not what I meant and you know it."

Fozzie growled from where he was laying in front of the refrigerator.

"Is this interrogation over? Because it's upsetting my dog." And I didn't much care for it either.

Steve slanted a scowl down at Fozzie. "I'm sure Cujo will get over it. As for his mom, I hope she'll accept the fact that there is nothing to be gained by spinning her wheels on a case that's been closed."

I knew there was wisdom in his words, but the road to acceptance felt like it was going to be a long and bumpy one. "I understand what you're saying, but—"

"The reality of a situation can be a hard thing to accept." A ghost of a smile faded from Steve's lips as he fingered a lock of hair that had escaped from my ponytail. "I know because I've been there more times than I'd like to count. It's just the way it is. We don't get to have all the answers."

I pressed myself into his arms. "I hate it when you

sound like the voice of reason."

"You just don't like to admit that I'm right."

That, too.

"So the wheel spinning is going to stop, right?" Steve asked, giving me his cop squint as he held me at arm's length.

"Of course." Depending upon what information Winnie could provide me.

I was raised by a grandfather who used to preach that it was better to ask forgiveness than permission.

That was right before he dug up two of Gram's flower beds to expand the back deck. It was his first major home improvement project after he retired. Because she didn't speak to him for two days, it also was the last project he launched without her blessing.

While I didn't require anyone's permission to have a chat with Winnie Dearborn, as a representative of the county I knew it was in my best interest to avoid all situations in which I had to ask for forgiveness. Especially after Shondra had made it abundantly clear that she was done looking into the matter of Ted Skerrett's death.

So on Wednesday morning, when I stepped through the third-floor office door and caught a glimpse of Shondra laughing about something with her assistant, I figured that I'd better take advantage of her good mood.

Fortunately, someone had started a pot of coffee prior to my arrival—always something that this caffeine addict appreciated. But it was especially timely this morning because it allowed me to stow my tote at my desk, grab my cup, and then head back to the breakroom to fill it and one of the clean spare mugs for Shondra.

"Knock, knock," I said after peeking into her office to make sure she wasn't on the phone.

Her piercing dark eyes zeroed in on the steaming mugs in my hands. "Is one of those for me?"

I took that as an invitation to come in and placed her coffee on a square of unoccupied wood grain between two stacks of files. "Thought you might like some fresh."

She reached for the mug. "Why do I have the feeling that you want to tell me something I don't want to hear?"

There was no point in beating around the bush, so I dropped into the chair across from her desk and met her wary gaze. "I learned something yesterday that I thought I should bring to your attention."

"This had better not be about Ted Skerrett."

"Well..."

"Are you hard of hearing? Because I specifically told you to leave that alone."

"I know, but I happened to meet up with someone who was in a romantic relationship with Mr. Skerrett."

Shondra frowned at me as she took a sip of coffee. "Unless this someone saw the guy take a header into that ravine, this conversation is gonna come to a rapid conclusion, 'cause I've got closing arguments today."

There was no way that I could portray Winnie as an eyewitness. Not unless she had more to tell about what happened on Friday. "I know she saw him on the day he died, and..." I didn't want to say that she broke up with him. It could sound too juvenile. Worse, too easy to dismiss. "They had some sort of emotionally charged exchange."

"Meaning what exactly?"

"I'd like to talk to her and find out."

"I don't doubt that for a minute."

"If nothing else, I figure she could help us with Mr. Skerrett's state of mind out on that trail."

Shondra set down her cup and shooed me away. "Go. Let me know if she has anything interesting to say."

I pushed out of my chair. "Will do."

"After that, we're done." She locked onto my gaze. "And when I say 'we' I mean *everyone* in this room. You got it?"

"Got it."

"Oh, and Charmaine," Shondra called out as I headed for the door. "Next time you want to sweeten the pot to get on my good side, I take two sugars."

Chapter Seven

WINNIE DEARBORN HADN'T sounded the least bit surprised when I called her to schedule an interview.

Since Shondra "I'm so done" Alexander wouldn't have crooked a pinky finger in the direction of her phone to tip off Winnie, I figured that Ted Skerrett's former lady friend must have a story to tell. But, three hours later, when I arrived at her Tudor brick home sitting atop the crest of the southern bluff overlooking Merritt Bay, I didn't expect that story to unfold in a formal dining room set for an English-style afternoon tea.

"Mrs. Dearborn, this is lovely," I said, admiring the skill with which my hostess had arranged the pink roses in the table's centerpiece to mirror the delicate rosebud pattern of the china place settings. "But you shouldn't have gone to so much trouble. As I said on the phone—"

"Nonsense." Winnie's focus shifted to the leaded-glass built-in cabinets that stretched to the ceiling. "I have shelves stacked with my mother's Royal Doulton—her prized possession when she came over from England after the war. This gives me a nice excuse to use it. Besides, it's lunchtime, and I'm sure you're hungry."

One of the junior prosecutors had asked me to sit in

on a late-morning witness interview, which dashed any hope I'd had of grabbing a quick salad prior to driving out here, so I was definitely hungry. But other than the innocuous slice of cucumber at the center of a half-dozen butter-laden finger sandwiches, I didn't see anything I could eat that wouldn't lead to me cursing at my scale tomorrow.

"Please, have a seat," Winnie said with a graceful wave toward the chair closest to a serving tray stacked with golden scones.

I slid onto an ivory jacquard-patterned seat cushion. "Everything looks wonderful." Especially the Devonshire cream and jam that had my salivary glands on high alert.

Winnie's kindly face flushed with pride. "Hopefully, it will taste that way. And, of course, I remember that you're a trained pastry chef, so I'll welcome your professional opinion of the scones."

Heck. As Winnie Dearborn's newly appointed food critic, I was now obligated to indulge. "I'm sure they're delicious."

She stood over me wearing the same nervous smile as my grandmother when the judges were sampling her cookies at the county fair.

I reached for the smallest scone on the tray, placed it on the dessert plate in front of me, and tore off a corner. "It breaks apart exactly as it should. Flaky, tender." I popped it into my mouth and almost felt my eyes roll back in my head as I savored the butterfat melting on my tongue. "Excellent."

Beaming, Winnie pushed the bowl of Devonshire cream toward me. "Just my humble opinion, but I think they're best with a healthy dollop of cream."

Even better, an unhealthy dollop. "But when a scone is perfect without it ..." I took another tiny bite to make my case. "You don't mess with perfection."

"My goodness." Fingering the top button of her navy and white striped tunic, she flushed again. "I dare say that I wasn't expecting to hear any happy news during this visit. Just shows that little moments of delight can happen at the most unexpected times."

She blew out a ragged breath, her eyes fixed in a vacant stare. "Quite unexpected."

I knew she wasn't referring to the high praise I'd been willing to offer to start this meeting off on the right foot.

Now, I needed to get her off her feet so that she would sit still for a few minutes. "Mrs. Dearborn—"

"Charmaine, you've known me forever, so let's make this meeting as pleasant as we can."

That explained the tea party.

She gave me a smile as brittle as spun sugar. "It's Winnie, please."

"Why don't you have a seat, Winnie." I pushed the bowl of clotted cream in her direction. "I surely can't eat this all myself." No matter how much I might want to.

She gave me a nod like she understood that it was time for us to actually start. "I just need to fix the tea," she said, stepping into a spacious kitchen. "English breakfast all right?"

I didn't particularly want any tea, but I knew that Winnie wouldn't relax until she had filled the pretty cup in front of me. "That's fine."

While she puttered in the next room, I admired the

mahogany sideboard sitting between the two lace-curtained windows I was facing. "That sideboard's a nice piece." I got up to take a closer look at its claw feet. "Another family heirloom?"

"My mother's," Winnie called out from the kitchen. "It doesn't really go with the table, but I couldn't bear to part with it."

I could see why. "It looks great there." And the carved cornucopia-edged backsplash provided the perfect background for the display of three framed photos placed at the center of a crocheted white table runner.

Recognizing Winnie's son holding a newborn in the center picture, I picked it up. "How's Ian doing?"

"You heard he lost his wife in a skiing accident."

"Yes. I was sorry to hear that." Not a day went by when Lucille didn't share some news about the latest birth, death, engagement, or divorce to impact the family of a Port Merritt resident. Typically, it's idle chatter about someone I barely know, just another snippet of gossip making rounds between the senior center and Duke's.

That wasn't the case the Christmas Eve I worked to give one of the waitresses the day off with her family, and Nadine arrived with the sad news. I knew Ian—not well, since he was two years ahead of me in high school. But he had impressed me as being kind and a little shy, and I liked him.

Okay, I'd had a tiny crush on him. Most of the girls in my circle of friends did. Ian was a cutie patootie. He was just too much of a nerd to realize it.

I returned the photo to the sideboard when Winnie

stepped through the doorway with a teapot. "Did I also hear that he moved back home?"

Pouring the tea, she focused intently on the cup she was targeting instead of answering.

Could his return home be a sore subject? "Sorry. Didn't mean to pry."

"You're not. I'm just not a very good multi-tasker," Winnie said, easing into her chair without making eye contact. "Now, you said you had some questions for me."

She obviously didn't want to talk about Ian.

Okay. We could come back to that.

"Yes. You mentioned yesterday that you had to break up with Ted Skerrett," I said, reclaiming my seat.

Taking her time to precisely slice a scone in two and slather each side with Devonshire cream, Winnie nodded. "Break up sounds a little melodramatic. I apologize for that. But yes, I told him that I didn't think we should see one another anymore."

"And why was that?"

Looking up from the jam she was spreading, she knit her brow. "Why is that of any concern?"

"We're just trying to get a sense of what had been going on in Mr. Skerrett's life."

"I see." She took a big bite and stared blankly at the centerpiece while she chewed.

Clearly, Winnie Dearborn didn't want anyone poking around in her personal life. I didn't blame her. I wouldn't want that either.

I nibbled on my scone to give her a little bit of time to think about the *why* question I was still waiting for her to answer.

She pushed the bowl of cream toward me. "I'm telling you, you're missing out if you don't try some."

Fine.

I slapped a big-enough mound on my plate to make my fat cells sing a hallelujah chorus. "So had you been seeing Mr. Skerrett very long?"

Winnie's cheeks reddened. "I hadn't been going behind Ruth's back, if that's what you mean. She was one of my best friends. The thought never would have crossed my mind."

"Sorry, I don't mean to imply anything. I'm just trying to understand the nature of your relationship."

Dropping everything to her plate, Winnie sat statue still. "He was a lovely man who asked me to lunch a couple of times. So, really, it was barely a relationship."

And yet, she *had* to break up with him.

"Are you saying then that Friday was the second time that you and Mr. Skerrett went out on a date?"

Winnie hugged her arms to her chest as she blinked back tears. "Seems silly to call them 'dates' at our age."

"Then let's call them 'get-togethers.'"

"Get-togethers," she said with a nod, as if satisfied with the sound of it to her own ears.

"In the last two weeks, how many times would you say you got together with Mr. Skerrett?"

"Seven. Maybe eight."

Wow. In the two weeks since Ruth's death? And they'd managed to keep this a secret?

"Most of those were to take walks together." Winnie smiled as she wiped away the tear trickling down her cheek. "He liked to go for walks, especially in the woods near his house."

My breath caught in my throat. "Woods. So like local

hiking trails?" Like Spirit Rim?

"Ted said being out in nature—amongst green, living things—helped him get through the pain of Ruth's death. Really, it helped both of us ... to just walk and talk."

"About what?"

"What to do next. You know, like living in the same house where there are so many memories. I had to make those same decisions after John died, so I tried to give Ted the benefit of my wisdom, for what it was worth."

"I'm sure you were very helpful."

"That had certainly been my intention—to help. I hadn't expected..." Winnie turned away, a quiver in her chin as she looked out the window.

Expected what? "To have feelings?" Because she obviously did.

"I shouldn't have let it go as far as I did."

"You enjoyed his company on those walks."

Winnie didn't say anything. Instead, she took a sip of tea.

"I'm sure he liked being with you, too," I said to give her a little nudge toward the marriage plans Lucille had mentioned to Alice and me.

Winnie set down her cup with an unsteady hand. "I'd thought so."

What was that supposed to mean? "You're not sure about how Mr. Skerrett felt about you?"

Her eyes welling with fresh tears, she shook her head.

"Did something happen last week to change things between you?"

She pressed her napkin to her eyes. "No. Nothing

happened."

Winnie had blocked most of her face with that darned napkin, but I didn't need a clear view of the worry tugging at the corners of her lips to know she was lying.

"Well, something must have happened for you to want to break things off with him."

"I...I just realized that things were moving too fast. That's all."

Maybe things were moving a little too quickly for her comfort zone, but that wasn't why she *had* to break up with Ted Skerrett.

"How did Ian feel about everything that was going on?"

Winnie blinked, tears cascading over mascara-free lashes. "He...wasn't...thrilled about it."

"So he knew about the walks and all the time you'd been spending together."

"Not at first, but yes."

"Did Ian worry that you and Mr. Skerrett were getting a little too serious?"

"Maybe."

That would be a yes. "And maybe he was the one who wanted you to slow things down."

"Only because he was concerned ..." Censoring herself again, Winnie reached into a pocket for a tissue and blew her nose.

"Concerned about the possibility that you might be rushing into something?"

After a moment of hesitation, I got another nod.

"How did Mr. Skerrett take it when you told him you couldn't see him anymore?"

"Not the way I had expected." She took off her glasses and dabbed her eyes. "Even though I tried to let him down gently, I thought he'd be crushed, especially after losing Ruth. But instead, he seemed more angry than hurt."

"Angry." That seemed like a strange reaction, but maybe Ted had been using some visible sign of anger to mask his feelings.

"Said that if I was going to reject him, I should have said so when he proposed up on the trail."

Holy crap. "The Spirit Rim trail?"

"We'd had a lot of long talks up there. It had become *our* place. We'd even had plans to go that evening." Winnie's shoulders slumped as she covered her face and sobbed. "But I ruined everything by breaking up with Ted…and…getting him killed."

Chapter Eight

"WHERE HAVE YOU been?" Patsy called after me when I tried to sneak by the third-floor hall monitor's desk around two.

Patsy and I both knew that she could make my work life miserable, so I pasted a smile on my face and braked to a stop. "Meeting. Did you need something?"

Pursing her lips, her steely gaze sharpened. "Yes. I need to know your whereabouts should Frankie ask."

I peeked into Frankie's office.

Empty, as I suspected it would be since Wednesday lunch meetings with the County Council often ran late.

This was nothing more than a power play, and I was in no mood for it. "Shondra knew where I was."

Patsy jutted her pointy chin at me. "Shondra's not Frankie."

And not someone who was angling for an excuse to rat me out to the boss. "Well, I'm here now."

She swiveled around to hand me a thin manila folder. "Then you can file this."

I didn't need to read the label. I recognized Ted Skerrett's file folder by the weight of it in my hand.

Patsy had resumed clicking on her keyboard, giving

me the none-too-subtle cue that I had been dismissed.

It didn't matter, I told myself as I headed down the threadbare hallway. I'd been dressed down—in English *and* Italian—by one of the worst kitchen czars I'd ever had the displeasure of working for. And he'd been my own father-in-law.

Patsy's daily dish of condescension was bland by comparison. Not that I wanted her to up her game.

As the lowest person on Frankie's administrative totem pole, I just needed to toe the line and do what I was told.

It was a no-brainer, right? If I wanted to continue collecting a paycheck, I had to follow each and every instruction I was given.

I had to be a good girl and tuck a file folder into the largest of the four black metal cabinets near my desk. It was Death Record Purgatory, where yellowing documents with the county seal waited for budget approval to be scanned and stored electronically.

In the meantime I was supposed to file it and forget about it.

Like that was remotely possible after everything I'd learned about Ted Skerrett's final days.

Maybe it had something to do with all the Devonshire cream and cucumber sandwiches I'd stuffed down my gullet while I waited for Winnie to stop crying, but my churning gut kept insisting that Ted's sister could be right.

"Ted didn't just fall off that ledge."

At least not without some help from someone who knew he'd be walking alone that evening.

Someone who would have known about Winnie's

breakup with Ted because he helped influence her to make that fateful decision.

I stopped in my tracks six feet from the bank of file cabinets hugging the windowless rear wall. "Ian!"

※

I needed more information than the county database I'd searched could tell me, so after work I drove a couple of blocks north to Eddie's Place, my favorite intel-gathering watering hole.

"Hey," my best friend Roxanne Fiske called out over the volume of the Bee Gees classic blasting through the speakers mounted over the massive oak bar. "You eating, drinking, or both?"

"Drinking, but nothing fun."

Resting a hand on her pregnant belly, she toasted me with her water bottle. "I'm right there with you, honey."

I ordered an iced tea and motioned toward the corner table in the mostly empty tavern. "Can you take a break for a few minutes?"

"Sure. We don't have any league action tonight, so Eddie should be able to cover the bar."

While she disappeared into the adjoining eight-lane bowling alley to find her husband, I took a seat and stared out the window at a lumber truck rumbling south in the late afternoon drizzle.

A very routine occurrence, especially the last few rainy days. But with all the bits and pieces I'd strung together to form a picture of everything that had led to Ted Skerrett tumbling into that ravine, nothing today felt especially routine.

"Char, are you okay?" Rox asked, sliding a tall icy glass with a straw in front of me.

"I was just thinking." I smiled at the sight of my favorite pregnant lady easing herself into a chair.

She blew out a sigh. "Whatever you're thinking, it'd better not have anything to do with me looking like I swallowed a beach ball."

"It doesn't. What do you know about Ian Dearborn?"

Rox blinked. "Well, that's not what I was expecting to hear. But it's funny that you should ask about him since he stopped by the other day."

"For a drink after work?" Because if that had been the case, I was going to have to come here more often.

"No, I think it would kind of be out his way since his practice is halfway to Gibson Lake."

And in close proximity to Spirit Rim.

"What practice would that be?" I asked, trying to sound only casually interested while my heart pounded in my chest.

"Didn't you hear the news from Donna? She was the one who spent the most time talking to him."

I shook my head. I hadn't seen our mutual gal pal in over a week.

"Turns out that Ian recently bought the veterinary clinic out on Route 104, so that should make Winnie happy to have family back in the area."

Maybe. It depended upon what that family member had been up to last Friday.

"And, of course, Donna is already scheming on him now that he's single again."

No surprise there. "And he's a doctor."

"Who loves animals." Pushing back a wayward lock

of chin-length caramel hair, Rox grinned. "The guy is going to have every single woman around here with a cat beating down his door."

"Probably true." But not what I wanted to talk about. "Any other scuttlebutt about him making the rounds?"

"Like what?"

"I don't know. Rumor mill stuff."

"Him moving back home after all these years has fueled some speculation about his daughter having some problems. You know, after losing her mom so suddenly."

"I'm sure. The last six months had to have been horrible for both of them. Take a real toll emotionally," I said, locking gazes with Rox. "Something that could change a guy." And strip away all the sweetness from the nerdy boy I used to know.

She pointed her index finger at me. "You're fishing for something."

"Who, me?"

"Yeah, you." Rox sucked in a breath. "You're not seriously considering..."

I didn't get the sense that she knew about my lunch meeting with Winnie Dearborn, but I wasn't ready for Rox to start playing detective with me and needed to get her off Ian's scent. "I'm just asking."

"Because you still have a crush on him."

What? "No!"

She waved me off. "I don't blame you. He's aged *very* well, don't you think?"

"I wouldn't know. I haven't seen him."

"If you'd come by more, maybe you would."

I ignored the little jab about my recent absence. "Life's a little crazy right now." I didn't want to explain why and sipped on my iced tea instead.

"That's funny. That's exactly word for word what Ian said when he came in to pick up his order Friday."

I practically choked on my drink. "Friday night?"

She nodded. "I almost sold his pizza to someone else. Thought he was gonna be a no-show, but turned out he was just running late. Some sort of issue at home."

I bet. "Do you remember what time that was?"

"Eddie was paying more attention to the baseball game on TV than the bar, so probably close to seven-thirty."

Which could have given Ian plenty of time to make a quick stop at Spirit Rim.

Rox cocked her head. "If you haven't seen Ian since he's been back, why are you asking all these questions?"

My mouth went dry along with my brain, so I peered into my glass as if a good evasive answer could be hiding under the ice cubes.

"Are you looking for a new vet for Fozzie?"

Perfect! Good save, Roxie. "Yeah, he growled at the last one."

"I don't know that he'll like Ian touching him any more than the last guy, but you might," she said with a chuckle.

"Stop it. I'm only interested in him professionally because Fozzie's been ... uh ... scratching his ear a lot lately." I'd only actually seen him do it once, but that seemed like a good reason to drag a healthy dog to a veterinary clinic.

Glancing over at Eddie giving her the high sign that she was needed back at the bar, Rox pushed out of her chair. "Sounds like you'd better make an appointment."

My thought exactly.

After I fed my furry roommate and took him on a long after-dinner walk, my phone buzzed with a text from my mother.

Want to show you something when you get here.

Huh?

I stared at the cryptic message.

The only interpretation that made any sense was that my mother was back at Gram's after spending a week in Los Angeles.

Marietta had played it up that she would be meeting with a producer who wanted her to make a guest appearance on his new cop show. This was with no mention of the name of the show or the producer, not at all consistent with how my name-dropping mother operated.

Clearly, she had been lying.

She'd already had her final fitting for the wedding dress that had been hanging in her closet for most of the last month, along with the voluminous designer ward-robe she'd shipped up from her house in Malibu.

She had just needed an excuse to be in LA for a week, and Gram and I both suspected it was because Marietta was getting a little "tune-up" prior to her wedding.

I appreciated the fact that my mom had the Marietta Moreau image to maintain, especially since lending her famous face to a line of cosmetics, but that didn't mean that I needed to hustle over to bear witness to the benefits of her chemical peel.

I texted her that I was busy and headed out my door to go grocery shopping instead.

My phone started ringing before I made it down the three flights of stairs to the parking lot. But to my great relief it was Steve. "Hey, are you home 'cause I'm on my way to the store and—"

"Since your grandmother has dinner ready, you might want to make a detour."

I had cancelled our standing Wednesday dinner dates with Gram two weeks earlier. She'd understood it was temporary—that I couldn't lose weight while she fed me heaping slabs of pot roast and gravy.

Okay, the heaping slabs were on me, not her. Same with her cheesy twice-baked potatoes I couldn't resist.

So no fat-laden, yummy dinners. No matter how much I craved them.

Gram knew that I needed to live yum-free for a while. So did Steve.

"What's going on?" I asked him as I crawled into my car.

"Would you like to ask your mother that question? Because she's right here and seems eager to talk to you."

Criminy. I hated it when he got dragged into my family crapola. Unfortunately, I knew that Steve hated it even more. "I'm on my way."

Less than ten minutes later, he gave me a quick peck on the lips when I stepped through my grandmother's back door.

"She's here," Gram announced, marching into the dining room with a serving dish full of cheesy potatoes.

I sighed at the mouthwatering sight of them. "Do we know what this is about yet?"

He shrugged. "All I know is what your mother said when I pulled into my driveway. She has some 'big news' she wanted me to hear."

I followed Gram to the stove, where she was filling a gravy boat. "You've obviously been cooking for the last couple of hours. Why am I just hearing about this now?"

"Your mother has been running around here like a chicken with its head cut off for most of the afternoon, so who knows. She asked me to make pot roast for dinner, so I put a roast in." Gram pushed the gravy boat into my hands. "Now get in there so we can eat and get whatever this is over with."

I glanced at Steve, standing behind me in the food receiving line. "Sorry you got roped into this. I promise that I'll try to get you out of here as soon as possible."

He smirked as Gram handed him a platter of sliced roast beef. "And miss all the fun?"

Some fun.

Girding my loins, I pasted a smile on my face when I saw my mother. "Hi. Sorry I kept you waiting. I didn't know about dinner until Steve called."

"I texted you," Marietta said, wrapping her arms around me the second I set the gravy boat on the table. "A couple hours ago."

"I never got it." Extricating myself from her musky jasmine embrace, I met the disapproving gaze of Barry Ferris, Marietta's soon-to-be fourth husband, and almost felt like I should have been handing my former high school teacher a hall pass. "Hey, Barry."

Without making the pretense that he had any desire

to attend this meeting that his fiancée had called to order, Barry reached for his almost-empty wineglass. "Charmaine."

"You never got it," Marietta said, crinkling her brow as much as her latest Botox treatment would allow. "How strange. Oh, I know. I probably never hit *send* because that was right when my real estate agent called." She sucked in a sharp breath. "Oops. I wasn't going to mention that until after dinner."

Since Barry didn't appear any happier with the spoiler that had just slipped from his betrothed's glossy lips, I kept my mouth shut.

Unlike Gram, whose jaw dropped. "What's going on, Mary Jo? Why do you have a real estate agent?"

The former Mary Jo Digby beamed. "We've bought a new house!"

Chapter Nine

"BUT BARRY, I thought you were remodeling your house so that it would be like new," Gram asked, passing him the potatoes.

"That was the plan." He jammed the serving fork into a potato as if he and his plan were beyond done, and handed the dish to Marietta.

"Indeed, Mama," she said, squeezing out a fake smile. "That *was* the plan, but it became obvious in the last month that we needed to rethink it."

By the anger etching a path between Barry's brows as he drowned his beef with gravy, I had a feeling that my mother was using the royal "we."

She reached across the table to pass me the potatoes. "I mean, really. The lack of privacy was going to be a problem."

"You would have the same amount of privacy there as you do here," Barry stated without looking at her.

She pursed her Cupid's bow mouth. "Must we go over this again?"

I leaned into Steve as I passed on my favorite cheesy carbs and whispered, "Signal when you want me to get you out of here."

He gave me a little nod. "No potato?"

"If I need some cheese, I'll have some of yours."

"The heck you will." He angled away from me, guarding his plate. "Get your own."

"Everything okay?" Gram asked, shooting me a nervous glance as the platter of pot roast came to rest in front of me.

"Everything's fine." At least on this side of the table.

I aimed my thumb at Steve. "Someone's just being ornery."

"Must be something in the water today," Marietta said on a sigh.

Barry turned to her. "I don't think I'm being unreasonable or ornery."

My mother set her fork down. "My darling, you've seen it yourself over the last few months. Fans are showing up at the house all the time."

Now it was Barry's turn to heave a sigh. "One. One guy followed us home after we stopped for ice cream in the DeLorean."

"And he wouldn't leave." She looked across the table at me like she needed an ally. "It was creepy."

Since this incident involved them joyriding in the same car that my mother drove thirty years ago on her TV show, I seriously doubted that she minded all the attention. After all, that had been the point of her making the occasional public appearance in the DeLorean—to keep that part of her fandom alive.

"He only wanted to talk about the car," Barry stated in the dispassionate monotone that used to put me to sleep in class.

"He kept looking over at me." She dismissively

flicked a gold-bangled wrist. "And it's happened more than once. That's when I realized that we needed to reconsider our housing situation. And not just here in Port Merritt."

Gram knit her brows. "Are you talking about your home in Malibu?"

"Officially on the market as of Monday, and should fetch a pretty penny. Celebrity homes usually do," Marietta said, reaching for her wineglass.

Since our resident actress had slipped off the Hollywood B-list over a decade ago, I doubted that the listing agent would consider the dregs of her celebrity cachet that much of a selling feature. But given the temperature in the room, it wasn't in my self-interest to appear less than agreeable. "I'm sure they do."

"So that's why you went to LA last week? To put your house on the market?" Gram glanced at me. "Because Char and I thought—"

"You were having some meetings down there," I interjected, because it was obvious from her taut, dewy skin that at least one stop had been at her aesthetician's.

Marietta picked up her fork, suddenly interested in her potato. "I was, and I thought they went rather well, but my primary concern was to meet with my real estate agent and get the house listed. Because I wanted to race back and start house-hunting as soon as possible."

Barry blew out a derisive breath. "Obviously."

My mother brightened as if she had to compensate for the sullen guy next to her. "And we found the perfect home on the bluff past 42nd Street. Wait 'til you see it, Mama. It's practically brand-new, and it has a gorgeous view of the bay. And of course, it's in a gated community and has a security system, so our privacy won't be an issue."

"I see." Gram pushed her plate away and folded her hands in front of her as if some parental discipline would be the next course. "It sounds lovely, but are you sure you're not rushing your decision?"

With a pretty pout, Marietta leaned back in her chair. "Quite sure."

"But, sweetheart ... now that you're in a slightly different position because you've cut back your work schedule..."

I knew Gram was tiptoeing around the landmine that Marietta had been privately bemoaning: that her agent hadn't called with a movie offer in over eight months.

"Don't you think it would be prudent to wait for one of the other houses to sell first?" Gram gently asked.

My mother's green eyes flashed fire. "Absolutely not. It's not like I need that money. *I have money.*"

"We," Barry interjected.

She patted his hand. "Of course, dear. That's what I meant to say."

Sure it was. "That's good, then, because it could take a while for the right buyer to come along in Malibu. In fact, didn't you tell me a while back that you wouldn't be able to afford it in today's market?"

"No," Marietta protested. "I most certainly did not."
Liar.

"I'm sure your house will sell quickly, Barry." Gram leaned in to give him a reassuring smile. "Once all the remodeling is done, of course."

He didn't seem to take kindly to Gram's effort to find a bright spot in tonight's big announcement. Instead, he gave me a hard stare as if a stint in detention could be in my immediate future.

What did I do?

"Actually, Mama, we have another plan for that house." Marietta pointed a manicured index finger at me. "Because we have an offer you'd be a fool to refuse."

"Your mother's right. That offer is a sweet deal," Steve said as we walked up the drive to his house two hours later.

"It's complicated enough that Barry Ferris is about to become my fourth stepfather. I don't need to make the situation worse by having him as a landlord."

"How many times have you had to talk to your current landlord?"

"I wouldn't do that 'cause there's a resident manager at my building. If there's a problem, I go to him."

"Okay," Steve said, unlocking his front door. "How many times have you had to do that since you moved in?"

"Never, but I'm not living in his apartment with his furniture." I followed Steve into the kitchen where he dropped his keys on the white tile counter. "The only thing the guy cares about is that I pay my rent on time." And I knew that wouldn't be the case with Barry. Not while I had a dog that was sure to scratch the newly refinished hardwood floors Marietta had been bragging about when she insisted that we all go over to Barry's house after dinner.

I took a seat at the kitchen table. "This 'sweet deal' has disaster written all over it."

"Your mother just wants you out of that seedy apartment."

I grimaced at him. "I beg your pardon. It's not *that* bad."

"Her words, not mine, and yes," he said, joining me at the table after pulling a beer from the refrigerator. "It is that bad."

"Okay, fine. It's no penthouse suite. I got it because the price was right and it was close to work."

"And your mom's offer is to let you live at the house rent-free, and you'd only be adding nine or ten blocks to your commute. Not to mention the fact that you'd be right down the street from the dog park."

"Stop helping. It's still an insane idea." I took a swig from his beer bottle.

"Is it? Or are you just being stubborn because the idea came from your mother?"

I handed him back the bottle. "I'm not being stubborn. I'm being practical." Because, clearly, I wasn't the Digby family member Barry had envisioned moving into his house.

"You'd be living rent-free in a nice house with a fenced yard for Cujo." Steve nodded. "Yeah, I can see why you wouldn't want to jump all over that."

"I told my mom I'd think about it."

"That usually means no."

"Hey, she's the impetuous one in the family, not me."

He gave me a lopsided grin. "Yeah, right."

"I just need a little time to think. There's a lot swirling around in my brain right now, and I wasn't expecting to have to make room for this craziness."

"Because there's so much other *crazy* going on in

there?"

I pushed out of my chair and gave him a kiss. "You really know how to sweet-talk a girl."

"It's a gift." Steve pulled me onto his lap. "Stick around and I'll sweet-talk you some more."

"I guess I don't have to leave just yet." I linked my fingers behind his neck. "Let the sweet-talking commence."

He kissed me long and deep, tasting of beer as his tongue explored mine. Just when my insides started to melt like chocolate over a flame, he pulled back to adjust how I was sitting on him.

"Cramping your style, was I?" I whispered in his ear right before I nibbled on his lobe.

"Okay, we're done here," Steve announced, pushing me to my feet.

"Is the sweet-talking over?"

Grabbing my hand, he marched me down the hall to his bedroom. "In a manner of speaking."

Goody.

Chapter Ten

"LAND SAKES, GIRL, you look like you were ridden hard and put away wet," Alice said, looking up from the apple she was paring when the kitchen door banged shut behind me.

"I took a shower." At three o'clock, when my restless mind wouldn't stop churning. "I should look fresh as a daisy." I stowed my tote in my old locker and grabbed a white apron from the nearby hook.

She squinted at me. "I've seen fresher."

Swell. "Thanks a lot."

Standing by his sizzling doughnut fryer, Duke watched me tie the apron around my waist. "You know that most of our paying customers don't feel the compunction to help prepare the food."

I smiled sweetly at the old coot. "I'm not your typical paying customer, now am I?"

He smirked. "Ain't that the truth. So are you here to work off your tab?"

If my great-uncle were being totally honest, he'd admit that I more than made up for the food I consumed. Usually when I needed to do some mindless baking, like this morning.

"Sure." I looked at the wall clock mounted above a vintage red and white Coca Cola sign. *Five-twenty.* "I'm yours for the next two hours, so put me to work."

Alice pulled a stainless steel mixing bowl from a shelf behind her and placed it on her work table along with her laminated recipe book. "Are you sure you're up for this, honey? You look like you didn't sleep a wink."

"I'm fine," I said, stifling a yawn. "What do you want? Cookies or muffins?"

"Suit yourself."

After making a quick trip to the coffee station for some industrial-strength wake-up juice, I rolled up my sleeves, washed my hands, and got to work at the other end of the butcher block table.

Flipping the pages to her bran muffin recipe, I glanced up to see my great-aunt giving me the worried look she usually reserved for Duke when she thought he was working too hard. "What?"

"It has to do with Ted Skerrett, doesn't it?" Alice asked.

I reached for the sack of flour at the center of the table. "What does?"

"Why you're not sleeping. I heard you in here yesterday. You think Ted killed himself."

"No. I just think it's weird—"

"It is weird. I sure wouldn't have thought he was capable of such a thing."

I knew I needed to choose my words carefully because they were sure to be repeated to Lucille when she got here in a half hour. "I guess."

"I mean over Winnie. Don't get me wrong, she's very nice, but—"

"But what?"

"It just doesn't compute, if you know what I mean."

"Yeah." I knew exactly what she meant and thought about that for several minutes while we worked in companionable silence. Because it didn't compute.

Nothing about the last couple of weeks of Ted Skerrett's life fit what I thought I knew about the guy.

"You've heard that Ted's service has been scheduled, right?" Alice asked, interrupting my thoughts while I poured batter into muffin tins.

"No." I hadn't been aware that it had been announced. "When is it?"

"Yesterday's *Gazette* said it'd be Sunday at one."

Steve and I had been invited to the Saturday wedding of a high school friend, but I hadn't made any plans for Sunday. Until now. "I think I can make it."

"Make it where?" Lucille asked as she hung up her rain-spattered jacket on the hook by the door.

"Sheesh, doesn't anybody sleep anymore?" Alice remarked.

Shaking her head a little, Lucille approached in her squeaky shoes. "I woke up thinking about Winnie."

My great-aunt shot me a sidelong glance. "Seems to be a lot of that going on."

Lucille slid onto the barstool next to me. "I have a theory."

"Of course you do," Duke chimed in as he fished his last batch of fritters from their oil bath.

She gave him a dirty look. "As I was saying before I was so rudely interrupted, I think I know why Ted took a header off that overlook."

"Why?" Alice and I asked in unison.

Lucille leaned in. "Debt. Had to have been drowning in it."

Alice scoffed. "Don't be ridiculous. Ruth was loaded."

"When they first got married." Lucille lowered her voice as if one of the other waitresses was around to overhear. "I heard they were spending like there was no tomorrow the last few months."

I'd heard the same thing from Brenda, who had explained it away as Ruth's decision after she got the news from her doctor about her very limited tomorrows. "I wouldn't jump to any conclusions."

"Given my long night of ponderin', I wouldn't say I was all that quick to jump," Lucille said. "But I think that's exactly what Ted did after Winnie cut him loose."

Alice stared slack-jawed at Lucille. "Holy smokes! Winnie. I hadn't made the connection."

Clearly, neither had I because I didn't understand what she was referring to.

"What *connection*?" I asked, watching Lucille and Alice nodding at one another.

Lucille aimed one of those nods my way. "The rich widow connection."

My heart pounded as if I'd mainlined a pot of Duke's coffee. "Winnie's that rich?" I'd been to her home and had seen that she was surrounded with nice things, but growing up, I'd never gotten the impression that Ian came from money.

Lucille's thin lips curled into a knowing smile. "Oh, yeah. Her father invented some sort of super seed back in the 1980s. Made a bundle and left her everything."

Holy smokes indeed! Winnie's wealth could explain Ted Skerrett's pedal to the metal courtship as well as

Ian's reaction when he heard about it.

"I bet Frankie didn't consider any of this when she signed Ted's death certificate," Lucille said to me.

I knew Lucille had some pretty good news sources, but most of them traveled the beauty parlor/senior center circuit, not the courthouse.

She was fishing. "I can't confirm or deny anything."

Lucille sighed. "Figures."

"Now if you'll excuse me," I said, scooting back from the table. "I have muffins to get into the oven."

"Not so fast, young lady."

I could hear Lucille's squeaky footsteps behind me. "You know that I can't talk about this stuff."

"Oh sure, clam up now that I've solved the case for you."

After popping the muffin tins into the industrial oven Alice wasn't using for her pies, I turned to face Duke's chief conspiracy theorist. "First of all, there is no case."

She scowled. "Come on. No one here thinks that good ol' Ted got a sudden case of the clumsies and fell into that ravine."

It didn't matter that I agreed with her. Admitting it would be like throwing water on a grease fire. I'd only be stoking the flames. "There is no case," I repeated. "And I doubt that Winnie would want to be the subject of any more speculation than she already is, so let's not talk about this with anybody else."

"Ah-ha! That's because you know I'm right. Why else would Ted take a flyin' leap?"

A son who wanted to protect his mother could have had something to do with it. Maybe even someone Ted owed money to.

I smiled sweetly. "I couldn't begin to guess."

"Bullpucky. You've been sniffin' for clues ever since Howie told you where they found the dude's body."

"Don't know why you'd think that, since *there is no case.*"

Lucille pursed her lips. "Really? That's the way you're gonna play this?"

"I got nothing for you, Lucille," I said walking back to where Alice had been keeping a watchful eye on us.

"You're not the only one around here who can tell when someone's lying, you know," Lucille barked at my back.

True, but I was counting on the fact that my *lie-dar* was a lot more reliable than hers.

Alice threw her pal a glance of reproof. "Time to give it a rest, Luce. You want to dig for more dirt, go to the funeral. That's what Char's gonna do."

I muttered an obscenity under my breath.

"Is she now?" Lucille sidled up next to me. "Case closed, my sweet bippy."

When Lucille wouldn't stop buzzing me like a hungry locust, I headed to the relative safety of the courthouse, where I kept an eye on the clock so that I could make an appointment for Fozzie when the veterinary hospital opened.

I was informed that we wouldn't be able to get in until late tomorrow, but that was okay. I didn't want to appear overeager to talk to Ian, especially if his mother had mentioned my visit to the house. I also needed some time to consider what I wanted to say after all these years.

Fortunately or unfortunately, Patsy provided me several hours of alone time when she delivered a tall stack of files that needed copying for an upcoming criminal case.

Just when I thought I had cleared my final paper jam of the day with the office's persnickety dinosaur of a copier, Shondra came in with a thick manila folder.

"Oh good, you're in here," she said.

That sounded like a reprieve from all the filing waiting for me when I got back to my desk. "Something I can do for you?"

Shondra handed me the folder. "I need two copies of everything."

Swell. "No problem."

She started for the door, and I thought I should mention my interview with Winnie Dearborn before Shondra rushed off to court. "Do you have a second?"

"I have a conference call in a few minutes, so make it fast."

"It's about the woman who was romantically involved with Ted Skerrett."

"You talked with her?" Shondra asked, glaring at the florescent light flickering above our heads like she wanted to shoot it.

"Yesterday."

"And?"

"There seemed to be some concern that Mr. Skerrett was only interested in her because of her money." I left out the part about that being the thrust of Lucille's argument. "Mrs. Dearborn, the widow he'd been seeing the two weeks prior to his death, said that he was pretty angry when she broke it off with him."

"That's it?"

I nodded. "There is one other thing that one of Mrs. Dearborn's friends mentioned—that Mr. Skerrett had run up some debt. Could certainly be a factor as to his state of mind Friday night."

Shondra shrugged. "Maybe. We'll probably never know."

So much for running Lucille's theory up the flagpole.

But maybe Shondra would be willing to consider it if I could supply more than a theory. "Maybe I should—"

"Nope." She stepped into the hallway. "Do you know why?"

I didn't need more than one guess. "Because we're done?"

"You got it," she said, leaving me alone with the flickering light and another hour of copying.

"Great." Sometimes I really hated being right.

Chapter Eleven

"STOP GROWLING LIKE you hate it here," I said to Fozzie as we drove through Mr. Ferris's neighborhood. "We're just looking."

I slowed to park in front of the 1930s butter yellow Craftsman bungalow I'd toured last night. "Admit it, it's pretty nice." Not quite nice enough for a mother with champagne taste. But I was more of a beer and wine girl, and the price of this charmer was beyond right.

"He'd still be my landlord."

But think of all the rent money you could save.

"No, I'd better insist on paying rent. I wouldn't want Mr. Ferris to think I was trying to take advantage of the situation."

Fozzie looked over and woofed.

"I know. I can't believe I'm even considering it."

He barked again, his toenails digging into my thigh as he lunged toward the driver's side window.

"Settle down," I said, glancing out to see a boxer on a leash across the street. "It's just another dog. Probably lives around here, so be nice. He could become your new neighbor." Maybe.

The petite woman walking the boxer was wearing

oversized sunglasses and a floppy white hat so I couldn't see her face. But I recognized the fringe of carrot red hair peeking out from under the hat—the other Gray Lady who'd had an entry in the Ted Skerrett sweepstakes: Carmen Majorino.

Shutting off the ignition, I reached into the back seat for Fozzie's leash. "Want to see if they're going to the dog park?" Because I sure did.

I'd given Fozzie a post-dinner walk before we left my apartment around six, so after he hopped out and left his mark on the same patch of weeds that the boxer in front of us had watered, I figured his reservoir should have been tapped out.

But once we stepped off the sidewalk, Fozzie promptly relieved himself on a spindly bush near the fenced entrance to the park. Probably because the other dog had done the exact same thing.

With Carmen's floppy hat in my sights, I gave his leash a tug. "This isn't a pissing match, you know."

Fozzie took a couple of steps, sniffing the dirt path like a bloodhound as he led me down the trail.

"Good job. You're on the scent." Me, too. Only it wasn't another dog I was chasing.

Closing fast while the boxer followed his nose at the base of a wooden bench, I tightened my hold and pulled up on Fozzie's leash. "Well, hello," I said, trying to sound casual.

Carmen turned, dipping her head to look over her sunglasses. "Charmaine, fancy meeting you here." She reached out a hand to the dog straining against his leash. "Who's your furry baby?"

"This is Fozzie. He can be a little skittish around

strangers." Especially with the boxer barking at him. "So you might not want to get too close."

Blood-orange lips rivaling her hair color parted in a friendly smile as she retrieved a dog biscuit from a pocket of her nylon windbreaker. "Oh, I don't think that will be a problem, because I have something that can make us instant friends."

While Fozzie crunched on the treat, Carmen stroked his ear. "There. You're not so tough to win over. If only men were so easy, eh, Charmaine?" she quipped with a rheumy chuckle as she tossed her own dog a biscuit.

I felt as if she were cracking open the door to the conversation I wanted to have with her, but I wasn't quite sure what to say when I stepped through. "Right."

"You come to the park often?"

"Not as often as I'd like. But we both need the exercise. So if it's not the park, we try to hit one of the local trails a couple of times a week."

Carmen pursed her mouth. "Not Bella and me. I got bad knees. I can handle the short walk to the park, but that's it."

Then she wouldn't have been joining Ted on any hiking trails.

"Do you mind if we sit for a minute to let our dogs get acquainted?" Not that they looked like they needed a lot of encouragement since Fozzie was having a get-acquainted session with Bella's butt, but I figured that this could buy me a few more minutes with Carmen.

"If that was a nice way to let an old lady get off her feet, thank you," Carmen said, easing herself down on the bench.

"Okay, busted. But I thought that you might be able

to help me with something that I heard at Duke's."

"Oh honey, don't believe everything you hear there." She pulled out two more little biscuits and threw them to the dogs. "Some of those old biddies are horrible gossips."

She should know. She was one of them.

"Isn't that the truth. It's just that one of them mentioned that you had been seeing Ted Skerrett before his unfortunate accident."

"I swear. Don't those girls have anything else to talk about?"

"It wasn't anything more than a passing remark. It just occurred to me that you might be able to help us with the timeline I'm putting together for the coroner."

And because the inquiry's closed, I sure hope you never mention this to anyone I work with.

Her back straightened. "Oh my. I don't know that I know all that much, but I'll try."

Good enough for me. "When did you last see Mr. Skerrett?"

"Friday. I was meeting Nadine for lunch and noticed Ted and Winnie going into Schmidt's."

"Winnie Dearborn?" I asked, trying to sound as if I were hearing this for the first time.

Carmen gave me another long look over her sunglasses. Only this time, her eyes were glistening with tears. "I know. I could hardly believe what I was seeing. After spending most of Monday afternoon in the kitchen to make the man the best Bolognese he'd ever tasted, I find out he's two-timing me with another woman."

"So you'd been seeing him for a while?"

"A while? Goodness, no. His wife had just passed, for

heaven's sake. It's just ..." She took her sunglasses off to wipe her eyes.

"You had feelings for him."

Carmen nodded.

Sheesh, this guy had been working fast.

"Had you two made any future plans?" I asked to find out if she also had that in common with Winnie.

"No. Ted had made it clear that he didn't want to rush into anything."

That Carmen knew about, anyway.

"I was okay with not rushing. I was happy to have someone to cook for." She winked. "Among other things."

With no desire to hear about anything beyond her kitchen, I tugged on Fozzie's leash to signal that it was time for us to make tracks for the exit. "Okay, that should be all the information I need."

Standing, I extended a hand to help her from the bench. "Thanks for your time, and Fozzie thanks you for the biscuits."

Carmen patted him on the head while he nosed her pocket with the doggy treats. "See? We're friends now. Just goes to show that the way to a man's heart is through his stomach."

In Fozzie's case, yes.

In Ted Skerrett's case, apparently not so much.

✳

Almost two hours later, Steve swung open his front door wearing just a towel low on his hips. "If you're here to take me to dinner, you're late. Plus, I'm not quite dressed for it."

"I'm not," I said as the door clicked shut behind me. But with the way his wet hair was curling, Steve looked good enough to eat. "I have something I want to run by you."

He hooked a finger into the V of my denim shirt and pulled me close. "Your body? Because it just so happens that I am dressed for that."

"Uh, no." With my palms on his solid chest, I put some space between us. "Fozzie and my groceries are in the car, so I can't stay long."

Steve grinned. "Who said we needed that much time?"

"There you go sweet-talking again."

"Hey, I told you—"

"I know. It's a gift." I pointed toward his bedroom. "Why don't you get dressed and let me do the talking."

"Something tells me that I'm not going to like what I hear," he muttered, disappearing into his room.

Probably.

Steve emerged less than a minute later in an old police academy T-shirt and blue jeans. "Okay, let's have it."

I followed him into his kitchen. "I've come into some information that makes me wonder if Frankie was too quick to sign Ted Skerrett's death certificate."

Opening a Corona, Steve gave me a hard stare. "I thought you were going to let this go."

"I was." More or less. "But Shondra wanted me to follow up with one last potential witness before she wrapped up the inquiry."

"I bet she did."

"Hey, it's important to be thorough."

"Uh-huh." He took a swig of beer.

"Anyway, it became clear after I spoke to this lady…" And Lucille. "That Ted must have been having some money problems."

Steve shrugged a shoulder. "Okay."

I inched closer. "I'm talking serious money problems. Like him needing to find another rich wife serious."

"And you think what? That this had something to do with him ending up dead?"

Yes! "Maybe."

"I assume you mentioned this to Shondra."

I nodded.

"Then you've fulfilled your duty, Deputy." He leveled his cop squint at me. "Now let this go."

"If you'd talked to all the people involved in Ted Skerrett's life the way I have, you might not be so quick to say that because…"

He was up to no good?

If I said that, Steve would pounce on me faster than Fozzie on a pork chop.

But between the screws Ted had been tightening on his late wife's children, and his rush to the altar with Winnie… "I'm pretty sure he was up to something."

"It's the way of the world, Chow Mein. Everybody's up to something. We're not all angels beneath our sugar coatings." Steve's lips curled into a dangerously sexy smile. "I speak from experience, because I'm one of the few."

I was about to challenge him on the veracity of his claim when he silenced me with a mind-numbing kiss.

Later. We could talk about this later.

Chapter Twelve

AFTER SPENDING MOST of Friday afternoon on the road to serve a subpoena on a witness who had moved to Big Lake, north of Everett, I had to hustle to make it on time to Fozzie's five-thirty appointment with Ian Dearborn.

Fozzie's nose was working overtime as we approached the red barn-like veterinary clinic opposite the berry farm on Route 104, so it didn't surprise me when he led me down a paved walkway to the door. But when I swung that glass door open and caught a whiff of antiseptic cleanser, Fozzie put on the brakes.

"I know," I said, taking him by the collar to coax him onto the ceramic tile of the waiting area. "You remember getting a shot at that other smelly clinic. I promise no shots today."

This is more for me than you.

After following a set of pink and blue paw prints to the receptionist's desk, where we checked in with a friendly twenty-something, I took a seat and completed the short form she had given me.

Five long minutes later with a restless Fozzie protesting the existence of the calico cat that had come in behind us, a pretty technician in kitty print scrubs escorted us back to an exam room with a metal table and light blue walls.

Introducing herself as Adrianne, she took my form, gave it a quick once-over, and then asked me to hold Fozzie by the midsection so that she could take his vitals.

"When did he last eat?" Adrianne asked, tucking away her stethoscope after listening to his heart.

All I could do was venture a guess since Lily, the ten-year-old I'd hired to walk Fozzie, would have been the one to give him a biscuit snack before she left my apartment. "Probably around three-thirty."

After weighing him, Adrianne reached for a digital thermometer. "And the scratching you indicated on your form seems to have been getting worse in the last week."

"Yes." And it was the only time I'd noticed it.

She lifted Fozzie's tail to insert the thermometer and he practically jumped out of his toenails.

I'm sorry. I'm sorry. I'm sorry.

"Will Dr. Dearborn be in to look at his ear?" Because I was going to get out of here and go buy my poor pup a steak if Ian didn't open that door in the next few seconds.

Giving me a cool smile, Adrianne patted Fozzie on the back. "I'm sure he'll be right in."

After she made a few notes at the counter, she invited us to make ourselves comfortable, and she padded away as noiseless as the kittens on her shirt.

Just as I was about to sit down, Fozzie whimpered with his head hung low.

"I really am sorry for getting you involved in this," I

said as the door opened and a six-foot-two veterinarian wearing a white lab coat and a disarming smile stepped in.

He extended his hand. "Hello, I'm Dr. Dearborn."

"I know." Standing palm to palm, I locked onto his gaze. "Hi, Ian."

He cocked his head as if he were searching his memory bank. Then his blue eyes widened and an attractive flush darkened the base tan of his cheeks. "Charmaine, right?"

"It's been a while." And I was packing around twenty more pounds since he'd last seen me.

"I saw Fozzie's last name, but I didn't make the connection," he said, picking up the clipboard Adrianne had left on the counter.

Ian had turned away from me, but he hadn't given off any indication that wasn't true. Along with his genuine surprise to see me, I knew it was safe to assume that his mother hadn't mentioned my visit to the house.

He glanced up as he scanned the form I'd completed. "So you moved back too, huh?"

"Almost a year ago. After a divorce."

Dang! Why did I mention that? It wasn't like I wanted my only suspect in Ted Skerrett's possible murder to think that I'd come to his clinic looking for a date.

Pressing his lips together, Ian nodded.

A clear pass on joining me in over-sharing land.

Understandable. His wife didn't leave him; she was taken from him.

"I was sorry to hear about the accident," I said before too many awkward seconds ticked by. "How's your daughter doing?"

"Doing great."

The fake smile he had flashed told me otherwise.

Ian put down the chart and turned his attention to Fozzie. "I think Peyton saw this guy when she and her grandmother were driving down Main Street a few days ago. She was very excited to tell me all about the 'bear cub' that she saw, especially since he was being walked by a girl she knew from school."

"I pay that girl to walk him. She had wanted to adopt Fozzie but her mother's allergic, so we worked out a way for her to spend time with him. And this way he's not alone in an apartment all day." I felt like I was over-sharing again, and it was making me more nervous than I already was.

What I needed to do was to get Ian talking about himself. "Well, you get the idea."

"I also get the name now," he said with a goofy chuckle, reminding me of the nerd I knew in high school. "Fozzie Bear, right?"

"I won't take credit for the name, but I think it fits."

Ian chucked Fozzie under the chin. "Let's check this little bear out, shall we?"

"It can take him a while to warm up, so don't be surprised if he growls at you." Even though Fozzie's curly tail was wagging.

"I don't think that'll be a problem," Ian said, lifting my sixty-pound fur ball to the examination table. "Dogs love me."

I could see why. A soft-spoken guy with kind eyes and gentle hands that provided soothing strokes while probing for irregularities.

"He's been scratching at his right ear?" Ian asked

while he shined a penlight into Fozzie's eyes.

"Off and on. Being a new dog mom, I wasn't sure if that was normal and thought it should be checked out." *By you, while I check you out.*

"Well, let's see what's going on." Ian motioned for me to stand next to him. "If you would, help keep him still."

While I locked my arms around Fozzie's ruff, Ian inserted an instrument into the ear in question.

I had to lean in to keep my fur ball from squirming, and in the process I ended up pressing my shoulder into Ian's arm. "Sorry if I'm crowding you," I muttered, way too aware of the heat coming off his sinewy triceps.

"No worries."

Easy for him to say. He wasn't the one with beads of sweat forming on his upper lip.

Ian put some separation between us as he looked through the instrument. "No sign of infection, and I don't see any indication of mites. What might be going on is a mild allergy."

He returned the scope to the counter, and while he did, I buried my face in my sleeve to do a quick mop up. "Like something environmental?"

"Could be. Pollen is a common factor."

"Well, there are a lot of things in bloom right now. In fact, we were on a hike not far from here and I thought I heard him sneeze."

Ian came back to the table and stroked Fozzie's ears. "His eyes and ears are both clear, so I wouldn't be overly concerned. And I would definitely continue those hikes, because this guy tipped the scales at sixty-seven pounds. Ideal for his size would be closer to sixty-two."

Great. It wasn't bad enough that I had to cut back on

the treats. Now my dog needed to join me.

"We'll work on that. In fact, as long as we're this close, we might as well hit Spirit Rim tonight," I said, watching Ian for a reaction.

The crow's feet surrounding his eyes deepened as he held my gaze. "That's a nice hike."

I wouldn't know, but I was quite certain that Ian didn't think it was so nice. "I hear the sunsets are great up there. When the weather's better, of course."

He glanced at a clock mounted near the door. "Yeah, but I wouldn't recommend heading out there this late. You'd be coming back in the dark."

"And I wouldn't want to be the next person to take a tumble from the trail."

His mouth quirked into a grim line. "No, that would be bad."

Bad? That's all he had to say?

I searched Ian's face to see if he had any more to offer.

Nothing.

Sheesh. This former nerd was either one cool cat, or he was quite adept at masking his emotions.

Easing back from what could become a dangerous precipice if I didn't stop staring, I ruffled the mane of black fur in front of me. "Looks like it'll be the dog park for you and me then, pal."

"Does Fozzie like the park?"

"Loves it."

"My daughter and I will be there Sunday. She wanted to go to the crafts fair a friend from school told her about, and I promised her a play date after."

Clearly, I wouldn't be seeing him at Ted Skerrett's

funeral.

Ian ran his hand over Fozzie's head, touching my fingertips in the process.

I stiffened, my heart pounding.

Sheesh. It's accidental contact. Cool it.

"If you'd like to join us, I know she'd like to meet the *bear*," Ian said while Fozzie's tail swept the table as if he knew we were talking about him.

"Sounds like fun."

"Three o'clock?"

I couldn't imagine that Ted's service would run much more than an hour. Even if it did, I didn't want to say no to this opportunity. "It's a date."

I mentally kicked myself as soon as the words popped out of my mouth. This wasn't a date. It was a chance to uncover the truth about what happened up on that trail.

It just felt like a date.

What *didn't* feel like a date was spending my evening alone with a snoring dog while Steve worked late, so I texted Donna to meet me at Eddie's for a girls' night out.

"Look who's gracing us with her presence," Rox called out over the din of the crowd at the bar as I headed over to join the stunning blonde waving at me. "And twice in one week."

I squeezed out a fake smile. "I was let out for good behavior."

"Hey, you," Donna said, giving me a warm, pear-scented hug. "It's been too long."

I slid onto the barstool next to her. "I know. Sorry

about that. Between Marietta's wedding and work, it's been a little nuts."

She flipped back a section of long hair that had fallen over her shoulder and I caught another whiff of ripe pear. "Are you wearing something new? You smell delicious." And she was making me hungry.

Donna's peaches and cream cheeks glowed with pride. "It's a new product line I'm selling at the shop. Doesn't it have the most fabulous scent?"

"I love it," Rox said as she spun a paper coaster in front of me. "Best shampoo ever. Wait 'til you try it."

With my mother lending her famous face to a competing beauty line, that could get complicated. And I didn't need any additional complications in our relationship.

"Char'll be doing that in a week when I do her hair for the wedding." Reaching out to inspect my split ends, Donna, the cosmetologist who owned the local cut and curl, clucked her tongue. "And it's high time, I might add."

I adjusted my ponytail to get it out of her reach. "I know. I'm long overdue to pay you a visit."

She slanted a disparaging glance at the back of my head while she sipped her wine. "You should let me cut that thing off. Be bold like the ten-year-old I had in my chair yesterday."

This sounded too much like the lecture she gave me back when she was attending cosmetology school, and I ended up going home with short, spiky hair like my mother's. After he had stopped laughing, my soon-to-be husband accused me of trying to look like a Marietta Moreau knockoff.

I wouldn't be making that mistake again.

"I happen to like this thing." I didn't, really, but at least pulling my hair back was easy.

I ordered a diet cola and Donna nudged my shoulder the second Rox stepped away. "You'll never guess who she was."

"Who?"

"The girl."

By the way Donna's eyes were sparkling, I was pretty sure I could guess. "Ian Dearborn's daughter."

Donna's jaw dropped. "How on earth did you—"

"I ran into him earlier today." Sort of. "And he mentioned that he had a daughter."

"Ran into who?" Rox asked, delivering my drink.

"Ian Dearborn." Donna leaned in, revealing several inches of décolletage above the V of her seafoam gauze top. "I had the pleasure when he was here last Friday."

And it looked like Donna was hoping that he'd be making a repeat appearance.

Rox cocked her head as if she were having trouble hearing us. "Char, are you saying that you took Fozzie in to see him already?"

I didn't care for how eager that made me sound. "They had an opening, and I thought I'd better grab it before someone else did."

Donna turned to me. "What's the matter with your doggy?"

"Nothing. The visit was more of a precaution than anything else." For me, not him. "It was good to see Ian, though."

Donna's lips stretched into a smirky grin while Rox slipped away to refill an empty pitcher for one of the tables behind us. "I bet it was."

"What's that supposed to mean?"

"I remember how you liked him."

"Me! You were the one who threw herself at him at the movie theater."

"I tripped," Donna protested, fluttering her spiky lashes.

"Yeah, right into his arms."

She heaved a sigh. "Didn't get me anywhere but upright. Still, it was worth a shot."

It struck me that Donna would have been one of the few people to have chatted up Ian shortly after Ted Skerrett fell to his death.

Taking her pulse on that more recent encounter was also worth a shot. "How did Ian seem to you last Friday?"

She shrugged. "Fine. A little reserved, I suppose, but that's nothing new. He was always on the quiet side."

"He didn't seem particularly nervous?"

"What? Around me?"

"In general." I tried to think of a behavior that wouldn't sound especially incriminating. "You know, like he was uncomfortable with looking you in the eye."

"Oh, he looked me in the eye." Donna pointed at her perky C cups. "Elsewhere too, so I don't think he was feeling overly uncomfortable."

Or particularly distraught. "I guess not."

"He just seemed like he was in a hurry to go. If it was something I said, I can't imagine what it would be."

"I'm sure it wasn't anything you said." Absolutely, positively sure.

Chapter Thirteen

"WHAT ARE YOU all dressed up for?" I asked my mother Saturday afternoon, when I arrived at Gram's and saw Marietta emerge from the bathroom in a curve-hugging lilac lace dress.

"The wedding. What do you think, silly?" She lifted a tapered index finger as she shuffled into my old bedroom on four-inch ankle strap sandals. "And I need just a couple more minutes, then I'll be ready to go."

I scowled at Gram as she descended the stairs in the teal two-piece dress she'd worn to the last two weddings we had attended. "Really? She barely knows Kelsey and Andy."

Annoyance tugged at the corners of her mouth. "What can I tell you? She wanted to go."

"Well, we'd better leave soon or we're gonna be late," I shouted up the stairs. "It starts at two."

While Marietta moaned about a missing earring, Gram retrieved her handbag from her kitchen table. "I'm ready. Where's Steve?"

"Waiting for us in his truck." Which would be sure to cramp my mother's style, so I texted him that we'd be driving Gram's SUV.

"Is there a problem?" he asked when I shut the front door behind him less than a minute later.

Yes, and her name was Marietta Moreau.

"My mother's coming with us."

His face darkened as if a shadow were passing over it. "Will this be happening sometime soon?"

"She just needs another minute, Stevie." Gram stepped in front of him and adjusted his navy pin-striped tie. "There. Now you look quite dapper."

He gave me a pointed stare. "Maybe someone needs to go up there and tell her to get her butt—"

"Why don't I see what's keeping her," I said, dashing up the stairs in a pair of pumps I had bought to go with my new floral print chiffon dress. Unfortunately, they were killing my feet and all my other shoes were a mile away.

I knocked on the open bedroom door and was almost overpowered by the cloud of musky jasmine hanging in the air. "Are we ready?"

The gorgeous creature with the cropped auburn hair turned to me dangling two different drop earrings from her fingers. "Which one goes best with this dress?"

Marietta already had pretty amethyst crescent moons hanging from her lobes, so I didn't understand why she was wasting time to take a poll. "The ones you're wearing are perfect."

She inspected her reflection in the dresser mirror. "Really? They seem a little underwhelming."

"They're fine." I picked up the clutch bag from the bed and handed it to her. "We need to go. Now."

Instead of moving, she squinted at me. "Speaking of underwhelming ... sugar, you look downright pale. Do you feel okay?"

"I'm fine. Let's—"

"If pictures are going to be taken, you're going to look all washed out."

"No one's going to be taking any pictures of us."

"I wouldn't be so sure about that," she said in a sing-song voice.

I headed for the stairs. "Trust me. Now, let's go!"

Almost two hours later, several Gray Ladies along with a bridesmaid lined the sidewalk with their phones aimed at Marietta as we approached the Port Merritt Country Club banquet room for the reception.

She shot me a sideways glance, her ruby lips curling with satisfaction. "Smile for the cameras, my pale darling who should have listened to her mother."

She and I both knew that they weren't lying in wait for me. Nor did they want me in their shots. "I'm going to wait for Steve. Wouldn't want him to think we abandoned him."

"He told us to go ahead while he parked the car," Gram said. "I'm sure he meant *all* of us."

Why should he be the only one to get a break from my mother?

"I'll catch up with you in a few minutes." I waved her toward the waiting paparazzi. "Go have fun. Alice and Lucille should be in there somewhere."

Gram shuffled toward the door like her feet hurt as much as mine. "Don't make me send a search party out to find you."

I figured that gave me a maximum of ten minutes

before Gram told Lucille to drag me in there, and I intended to spend each and every one alone with the great-looking detective heading in my direction.

At least that was my intention before I spotted Brenda Proctor getting out of her brother's pearly white Cadillac with a gift-wrapped box in her hand.

"Looking for a wedding date?" Steve asked me as he sidestepped one of the bouquets of balloons bordering the sidewalk.

I hooked my arm through his while keeping an eye on Brenda. "I was."

"Something change your mind?" He looked back over his shoulder. "Who's that in the parking lot?"

"Ted Skerrett's sister."

After an unintelligible grunt, he pointed toward the open French doors of the banquet room. "Shall we?"

My dogs may have been barking, but I had no intention of going in to give them any relief. Not until I had some answers.

"What do you think she's doing here?" Because I couldn't imagine that Brenda was a close friend of any member of the wedding party.

"The safe bet is that she was invited. In any case, it's no business of yours."

But it sure appeared to be the business of Mitzi Falco Walther, the mother of the groom, who was hurtling toward the parking lot like a steamroller in overdrive.

"You have your nerve showing up here," she shouted.

"Mom," her youngest son, Nate, called after her. "It's okay."

Steve pulled me close. "I think this is a family matter that doesn't need an audience."

Was he kidding?

I stepped forward and offered Nate a sympathetic smile. "Is there something we could help with?"

Nate shook his head, his cheeks flushed like his mother's, but for what I suspected was a different reason. "I wish."

I glanced behind us at the growing crowd of onlookers. "Should Steve ask that woman to leave before this attracts more attention?"

Tightening his grip on me, Steve whispered my name like a warning.

I patted his arm. *I know you're not thrilled with me volunteering your crowd control services.* But with Mitzi's volume increasing in the parking lot, his irritation was the least of my concerns. "I'm sure he wouldn't mind."

Nate muttered an obscenity. "I'll handle it. I'm the one who delivered the invitation."

Three hours later, I was pulling out of the country club parking lot when my grandmother poked me in the arm. "Spill it," she demanded.

I had avoided the topic of Mitzi Walther ever since I followed her and Nate into the banquet room, and saw no reason to change course now. Especially with Steve sitting next to Gram in the back seat. "About that debonair man I was dancing with?"

Marietta snorted, a clear sign she'd had too much champagne. "Oh, yes. Stanley's a regular Fred Astaire."

Gram poked me again. "Never mind Stanley. What

was the fight about in the parking lot?"

"There was a fight?" Marietta asked, looking back over her shoulder. "When was this?"

I glanced into the rearview mirror and met the hard as onyx gaze of my favorite detective.

Yes, I know. Change the subject. "I don't know what you're talking about. Who's hungry?"

Gram heaved a sigh. "You just ate."

"Two little meatballs." And half a piece of cake that I didn't want to admit to. "I could go for a big salad when we get to the house. Who's with me?"

Marietta flipped down the mirrored visor and applied a fresh coat of glossy lipstick. "Not me. Barry and I are going out. You know what that means," she said, smacking her lips.

I wasn't sure that I wanted to think about what that meant.

Flipping the visor back up, she settled in her seat with an expectant look on her perfect face as if it were story time. "You need to start talking."

"Yeah," Gram chimed in. "Something obviously happened, 'cause it's all that Lucille and Alice were buzzing about."

"You know how those ladies can blow the tiniest thing out of proportion." Not my best evasive maneuver, but it was at least rooted in fact.

"Ah-ha!" Gram gave me another poke. "Then something did happen in that parking lot."

Definitely not my best evasive maneuver.

"I'm sure it was just a misunderstanding, Eleanor," Steve told her.

She clucked her tongue. "I don't know why everyone's being so mysterious about this."

I didn't have any answers for her, and I'd been there to witness Mitzi and Brenda trading barbs in the parking lot like rival roller derby queens.

"Me either, Mama. Mah goodness, fights break out at weddings all the time," Marietta said, using her public persona Tupelo honey accent. "And it's not always a bad thing. Take the one that got written into the series finale of *Peachtree Girls*. The writers made it so romantic with Tom crashing mah wedding and punchin' the guy who'd kidnapped me to force me to marry him. Then Tom took me into his arms and carried me to his car, where he declared his love."

She hugged herself. "It was my best screen kiss ever."

Gram patted Marietta on the shoulder. "Sweetheart, I think you were the only wedding crasher today, but that was a nice story."

My mother sniffed with annoyance. "I'm sure there were some other extended family members in attendance."

I could think of one: Brenda Proctor.

"Probably," Gram said. "Although I can't imagine why any one of them would want to get into a dust-up with Mitzi."

My grandmother had cast her musing in front of me like a juicy worm on a hook, but I wasn't about to take the bait. Not while I could feel Steve drilling a hole into the back of my head. "I'm sure I wouldn't know."

She scowled at my reflection in the rearview mirror as I drove past Broward Park. "I bet."

"Oh," Marietta said, pointing at a teenage girl walking a dachshund. "I forgot about the dog park being four blocks away from Barry's house. Another excellent reason for you to move there."

I clenched my fingers around the steering wheel. "I'm well aware of that. Thank you."

She turned to me. "No pressure, of course."

Of course not.

"She's thinking about it, aren't you, Charmaine," Steve added.

I shot him a dirty look in the mirror.

He grinned, clearly happy with the change of subject.

"It's under consideration," I said, taking the right on G Street.

"Honestly, Chahmaine, I don't know why you're even hesitating."

"It's a big decision." One that came with blinking warning signs advising me to proceed with caution.

"What's to decide?" Marietta asked, dropping the fake accent as we approached Gram's house. "It's in a better neighborhood, it would give you more space, and it's free."

In the words of the grandfather who had raised me, *There ain't no such thing as a free lunch.* It was probably safe to assume that he would apply the same healthy dose of skepticism to free houses, too.

"I said I'd think about it, and I meant it." I pulled into the carport and killed the ignition. "Okay?"

"Fine," Marietta muttered. "Be stubborn."

"Now, girls, it's been a lovely day," Gram said. "Don't be snippy. Charmaine, are you coming in for that salad?"

I had lettuce at my apartment, where there would be no mother to hassle me. "Better not. I have a dog that's probably getting desperate for a potty break."

Just as I was about to escape the musky jasmine assaulting my sinuses, Marietta flashed me a saccharine smile. "If you only had a house with a fenced yard."

Chapter Fourteen

"FIGURES IT WOULD rain today," Gram said, folding her umbrella as we followed a heavy-set man I didn't recognize into the foyer of Tolliver's Funeral Home. "Makes this seem like a repeat of Ruthie's service."

I knew what Gram meant. The gray pall hanging over the town had given me an eerie sense of déjà vu as we drove here, and wearing my black funeral suit twice in three weeks only served to drive the point home.

This felt weird.

I scanned the rows of the 120-seat chapel and was surprised to see so many unoccupied chairs, a sharp contrast to Mrs. Skerrett's standing-room-only service at the nearby Lutheran church.

Even more surprising, Lucille and Alice weren't here. "Are we early?"

"Not at all," said Curtis Tolliver, the funeral director, stepping to the chapel door like a maître d'. He handed us each a program with a nice picture of Ted on the cover, and made a gesture of invitation toward the tapered candles flickering at the other end of the chapel. "We'll be starting shortly."

"Where is everyone?" I whispered to Gram as we

walked down the center aisle to what sounded like the lilting strains of the same string quartet we'd heard prior to yesterday's wedding ceremony.

"Maybe the rain held them up." She took a seat two rows back from Winnie and Nadine.

It was little more than a steady drizzle, so I knew that couldn't account for Lucille's delay. Something else was going on. "Maybe."

I took the aisle seat and surveyed the room. To my surprise I saw Nate Falco near the back, in the same row as the stranger we had followed in here.

I leaned into Gram. "Do you know that guy back there?"

She looked over her shoulder. "Mitzi's boy?"

Since I'd spent almost half my life sharing the same school grounds as Nate, I stifled a sigh. "No, the man with the bowtie that we followed in here."

Gram took another look. "Never seen him before."

"We miss anything?" Lucille asked, appearing out of nowhere to nudge me in the shoulder to make room for her and Alice.

I shook my head as I stepped into the aisle to let my great-aunt sit next to Gram, who had moved over two seats. "Where have you been?"

"Don't ask," Alice grumbled.

Lucille waved her away as she claimed the aisle seat. "Don't be such a sourpuss. Just because it didn't pan out doesn't mean it wasn't worth going."

I didn't have a clue what she was talking about. "Where?"

Lucille gave me a conspiratorial nod. "The senior center. There's a noon class on Sunday that some of the girls attend. Thought they might know somethin' about who Mitzi had that beef with yesterday."

"Nothing, huh?"

"Nada."

Good. That meant that none of the onlookers of the brouhaha had been able to identify the other woman as Ted's sister, Brenda.

"It was a complete waste of time," Alice groused in my other ear. "I kept telling her that the other woman would probably be here."

Alice had no idea how right she was, except for the fact that there was no "probably" about it.

I made a show of looking around as Carmen and two of her Gray Lady pals stepped into the chapel. "I don't see any ladies I wouldn't expect to be here. Although I am surprised there's not a bigger crowd."

"I'm not," Lucille said, waving at the ladies as they took seats in front of us. "Ruth was the popular one—all those committees she served on, the luncheons at the library that she had us cater. Everyone loved her." She lowered her voice as she snuck a glance at Carmen. "Ted was...well, you know."

Loved by some and despised by others?

Yep, that had been made crystal clear to me this week.

Lucille elbowed me as a brunette in a midnight blue sheath led a pair of teenagers to the empty seats across the aisle from Winnie. "Isn't that Ruth's daughter?"

"Holly," I whispered. I looked back to see if Marc would be joining her, but only saw Curtis at the door. "Hmmm."

"Yeah, I second that *hmmm*. I thought there was bad

blood between her and Ted."

"Why would you think that?" I asked to find out how much Lucille really knew about the feud over Ruth's assets.

"Just the impression I got from Ruth years ago, but maybe the kids and Ted made peace at Ruthie's funeral."

"Maybe." Not.

Lucille leaned into me as she craned her neck to look behind her. "Who's the pudge sitting six, seven rows back? The one in the bowtie a few seats over from Nate."

"Don't know. My grandmother didn't recognize him, either."

Lucille tapped Carmen on the shoulder and asked her the same question in a stage whisper loud enough for half the chapel to hear.

Turning in her seat, Carmen put on the glasses hanging from a chain around her neck. "Never seen him before."

I cringed. If the guy didn't know we'd been sneaking peeks at him before, he sure knew now.

"Oh, look, it's Mitzi," Carmen said with a friendly wave.

"What?!" Lucille and I turned as if our heads were on a swivel.

Mitzi Falco Walther was the last person I had expected to be in attendance, especially after the shouting match she'd had with Ted's sister.

"Hunh." Sitting on the edge of her chair, Lucille looked past me at Alice. "I figured she and her husband would've headed home to Bremerton after the reception ended."

Alice exchanged glances with Gram. "I guess we

shouldn't be surprised."

They clearly knew something Lucille didn't. "Why?"

"I'll tell you later," Gram mouthed to me.

Really? It was so big that she didn't want to risk being overheard?

"Tell me *what* later?" I whispered into Alice's ear as the string concerto recording came to an end and Mrs. Fleming took a seat at the organ stationed to the right of the lace-covered table with the alabaster urn.

Alice leaned into me. "Ted Skerrett and Mitzi had an affair back in the day."

Holy crap!

"She even left her husband for him."

When I was eleven or twelve, I heard the story about Mitzi running off with some friend of Gil Falco's after draining their joint bank account. At the time it was to help explain why Nate's mom wasn't around.

But I'd never known the name of the guy, not until today.

"Don't know why they didn't get married. Must have been a reason, 'cause I'm quite sure that was the plan," Alice added, her voice rising above the melancholy notes of the organ.

With the way Mitzi was looking daggers at the woman taking her seat in the front row, I was quite sure the reason's name was Brenda.

After the service, Lucille turned to me while we waited for the rows in front of us to empty into the center aisle. "You staying for the reception? You know." She winked. "To do some reconnaissance."

"Yep. But I happen to be staying for the cake," I said, looking over her shoulder at Nate sitting by himself.

It seemed that Mitzi had made herself scarce before she and Brenda could engage in a repeat of yesterday's confrontation. But the mystery man had gotten to his feet and appeared to be saying something to Brenda as Curtis escorted her out of the chapel.

Since the man looked a lot like a guy trying to hail a cab during a thunderstorm, I didn't think it was to offer his consolations.

"Cake," scoffed Lucille. "Well, I'm gonna ask around. See what I can find out about the big dude you were just looking at."

"Excuse me. I was looking at Nate and thinking that I should say hello to him."

"Yeah, right. Because it's been such a long time since the wedding."

"Because he's an old friend, and I hardly got a chance to talk to him yesterday," I said, observing a tearful Winnie step into the aisle to give Holly a warm hug.

Alice heaved a sigh. "Poor Winnie. She's taking this so hard."

"She had been very close to Ruth and the kids," Gram added as Nadine stepped up to say something to Holly. "Nadine, too. It's just tragic for the family to go through this again so soon."

One might reasonably think that, but Holly didn't look that broken up about it.

Lucille pulled me into the aisle. "The guy's on the move. Want to go get that cake now?"

Angling around the crowd in front of me, I spotted a

wide swath of worsted wool disappear into the foyer. "I could use a little cake. Just to keep my strength up."

Hooking her arm with mine, Lucille charged toward the door, where Curtis Tolliver was standing like a theater usher. "You're taller. You see him?"

"Not yet." But he couldn't have gone far.

"Ladies," Curtis said, inviting us to join the others in the reception room across from the chapel.

"There he is." Ignoring Curtis, Lucille dragged me to a long table with a punchbowl and paper cups as if she had worked up a powerful thirst, and cocked her head toward the man approaching Brenda Proctor. "We may not know who he is, but she sure does."

True, and since Brenda looked like a live grenade was heading her way, I felt like an explosion was imminent.

"What are you doing here?" we heard her demand as he closed the distance between them.

"You haven't been taking my calls," he responded in a clipped tone. "So you didn't leave me much choice."

Red-faced, Brenda turned as if they dared not be seen together. A second later, they moved to the far corner.

"Dang!" Lucille picked up two cups and filled them with fruity punch. "What do you think that was about?"

"No idea." But my first guess would be that it was another family squabble.

Lucille handed me one of the cups. "Who is she to Ted? A sister?"

"His twin, Brenda."

"Twin, huh? And maybe his only immediate family, so the big guy could be puttin' the squeeze on her to make good on her brother's debts."

"'The squeeze'?" a female voice behind me said. "Don't think I've heard that term outside of old gangster movies."

"Sorry." I stepped aside to give Holly access to the punchbowl. "We were just ..." There wasn't any positive spin I could put on what she'd overheard. "You know."

Holly aimed a smirk at the corner. "You were wondering what the *conference* over there is about."

"You betcha," Lucille said, answering for me.

Ted's stepdaughter passed two cups of punch to her kids. "Go get some cake," she told them. "I'll be there in a minute."

The second the teens turned their backs, Holly met my gaze. "Remember me telling you that a couple of appraisers were at the house that Friday?"

I nodded.

She thumbed in the direction of the man raising his voice in the corner. "He was one of them."

"Really. Any idea why she would have been avoiding him?"

Holly's mouth compressed into a tight line. "I'm sure Brenda's just being difficult about something. She won't even let me stop by later to move out some of the dolls. I was hoping she'd be less disagreeable today, but there seems to be some sport in letting Marc and me twist in the wind."

"Guess I was wrong about who's putting the squeeze on who," Lucille said while I watched Holly join her kids.

I didn't know that any squeezing was going on other than what Brenda and Ted had been doing to keep control of whatever was left of Ruth's fortune.

If anyone might know, I figured it would be the appraiser Brenda had just left standing red-faced in the corner. And since he was heading right for me, I knew I needed to act fast.

"Excuse me," I said, stepping into his path. "I wonder if I could run something by you."

Shaking his head, he pulled his handkerchief from his breast pocket and wiped his sweaty brow. "Actually, I was just—"

"Someone mentioned that you do estate appraisals."

He cast a wary glance over his shoulder at Brenda as she chatted with Winnie and Nadine. "What is this about?"

"I know that this isn't the place to get into this, but my grandfather passed away recently and left me his collection of Civil War memorabilia." He didn't, but Gramps had mentioned his brother's collection enough times that it was the first thing that popped into my mind. "And I'd like to know what it's worth."

His hooded eyes brightened with interest. "You're looking to sell it?"

"Seems like that would be better than to keep it in a storage unit."

He pulled out his wallet and retrieved a business card. "Why don't you give me a call and we'll schedule an appraisal of the collection."

I read the name on the card he had handed me. *Lawrence Ivie.* Yep. The same name that Brenda had given me earlier in the week. "I'll do that. Thank you, Mr. Ivie."

With a slight bow at his thick waist, he gave me a warm handshake. "I look forward to hearing from you."

Oh, I promise that you will.

Chapter Fifteen

AN HOUR LATER, Fozzie and I were following our noses to a food truck that had set up near Broward Park's picnic area, where several vendors were busy boxing their wares and folding canvas tents.

I suspected they were taking advantage of the break from the rain and wanted to get to their vehicles before the next band of showers started.

Wanting much the same thing, I scanned the grounds and saw lots of familiar faces, but no hunky veterinarian.

"Are we late?" I asked Fozzie.

Crap. Maybe I had spent too much time primping in front of my bathroom mirror for this non-date.

I was about to check the time when I heard a young voice shrieking Fozzie's name.

I didn't need to look to know that it was my dog-walker, Lily Maxwell, running in our direction. I could tell by the way Fozzie was bouncing at the end of his leash like a kangaroo at the sight of his favorite human.

"Hi, guys," I said, careful to focus my attention on Lily and the pretty little girl by her side instead of Ian, who was walking several paces behind.

"He does. He looks just like a little bear," the girl told her father while Lily wrapped her arms around Fozzie's neck.

Lily planted a kiss on the top of his head. "That's why he's called Fozzie, for 'Fozzie Bear.'"

I noticed the girl kept toeing the damp grass with her sparkly sneakers, her eyes gleaming while she watched Lily. If she was waiting for an invitation, with Fozzie sniffing the air between them, he was as good as saying that she didn't need to wait. "You can pet him if you'd like."

Ian put his hand on her thin shoulder. "Peyton, hold out your hand and I bet he'll lick it."

She opened her palm and Fozzie ran his black tongue over each one of her fingers. Giggling, Peyton looked up to her father. "He likes me."

Ian grinned. "He sure does. And you taste like cotton candy." He turned that devastating smile on me and my heart started beating double time. "An obvious winning combination."

"He likes the sweet stuff." Especially when it came in the form of cute, little brown-haired girls. "Would you like to take him for a walk in the dog park?"

Peyton's face lit up. "Can we?"

"Sure," Ian said while Lily took the leash from my hand and started running. "Just stay together, and say thank you to Ms. Digby before you forget all your manners."

Shouting a dutiful thank-you, Peyton ran off to catch up with Lily and Fozzie, almost bumping into Carmen, who was staring at me from the entrance of the dog park.

Uh-oh. I didn't need this meeting getting back to Lucille, or worse, Steve.

Pretending I didn't see Carmen, I pointed at the tree-lined playground that Ian and the girls had walked from. "Want to do a little loop of the park while we wait for their return? Knowing how much Lily loves that dog, it'll be a while." With any luck, long enough for me to extract a little information from Fozzie's new vet.

Ian smiled as we set off on the gravel-covered path that circled the six-acre park. "Lily was telling us that she walks Fozzie almost every day."

"It's a good arrangement. It makes her happy to spend time with him, and he gets an afternoon bathroom break so I don't have to rush home from work."

"What do you do?"

I didn't want to raise any suspicions by telling him. "I do admin work for the county." True enough.

Ian nodded as if I had revealed enough information to satisfy his curiosity. I also took that as an indication that Winnie hadn't mentioned my visit to the house.

"Peyton's a cutie," I said as we passed a couple of moms pushing their toddlers on a swing set.

"Takes after her mother."

I wasn't so sure about that. She had his dark coloring and enviably thick eyelashes. "Speaking of mothers, how is yours doing?"

He blew out a breath. "She was getting ready for a funeral when Peyton and I left, so I'm sure she's had better days."

"Ted Skerrett's funeral, right?"

Ian gave me a sideways glance. "Did you know him?"

"A little from working at Duke's. Strange how he

died, isn't it?"

"Yeah." Ian pressed his lips together as if he didn't want the thoughts furrowing his brow to slip out.

"I mean the timing. He's in town for lunch with your mom and—"

"How did you know about that?" Ian asked, stopping so abruptly that gravel skittered at his feet.

The storm clouds darkening his blue eyes told me I'd scored a direct hit to a sensitive nerve. "Have you forgotten how the rumor mill works around here? Nothing happens in the romance department that doesn't make its way back to Duke's."

Ian set off on the path. "Romance. Right."

I scurried to catch up with him. "Sorry, I didn't mean to imply..."

"Don't worry about it. I know people talk."

I kept my mouth shut as we walked, hoping that he'd elaborate to make up for my silence.

"It's just that life hasn't been easy lately for my mom," he finally said. "Peyton and I move in and disrupt her routine, and then Ted Skerrett makes a move of his own and burrows under her skin like a tick."

"What do you mean?" That Ted was a parasite that needed to be removed?

"I'm just saying that my mother deserves better."

With my heart in my throat, I touched Ian's arm so that he would stop and look at me. "Is that what you told him?" *Up on that overlook.*

He blinked with nothing more than mild surprise widening his eyes. "Told him? No, it's what I told her. Probably the most awkward conversation I've ever had with my mother since she tried to tell me about the birds and the bees."

Oh.

"I just hope that the funeral service today gives her some closure," he said as we rounded the tall Douglas fir near the eastern border of the park.

"I'm sure it will." Even though it didn't give me any, nor was this walk helping to close the book on the Ted Skerrett murder mystery.

If anything, I felt like I had taken a giant misstep, the only side benefit of which was getting to know my high school crush a little better.

Ian smiled as if he could read my thoughts, and I felt the old twinge in my solar plexus, the one that had been lying dormant for almost twenty years.

Oh, no. That is not happening.

The torch I used to carry for this guy needed to stay extinguished.

He waved at his daughter running toward us with Fozzie leading the way, and I realized that was where his focus had been just now, effectively throwing a bucket of ice water on my old torch.

"How'd it go?" Ian asked her.

Peyton beamed, slightly breathless. "Great! Lily and I took turns walking Fozzie, and then when she had to go home, he and I decided to run all the way back."

I shook my finger at him while he danced at her feet. "Don't get any ideas for next time we come here, 'cause I can't run that fast."

She gave the dog a big, squeezy hug. "I'll run with you anytime you want."

"You made a little girl very happy today." Ian pressed his hand in mine, his voice low. "Thank you."

"My pleasure," I said, trying to ignore the burn in my cheeks as that torch threatened to flicker back to life.

"Who's that?" Peyton asked, looking back at the carrot-topped lady waving at us as she left the dog park with her boxer.

Trouble.

✳

"Oh, no!" I yelled when I saw that I'd slept past the alarm I'd set for six o'clock.

I threw on some sweats to take Fozzie on a quick walk, and then did the bare minimum in the hair and makeup department so that I could arrive at Duke's before Carmen and her big mouth.

"How's it going?" I asked Aunt Alice when I stepped through the kitchen door ten minutes later.

"Fine." She barely glanced up from the dough she was kneading. "Typical for a Monday morning."

Typical was good. That meant that I had arrived in time to quash any tidbits of gossip about me and Ian that Carmen and her Gray Ladies crew might want to chew on.

I just needed a few minutes alone with Lucille so that she'd be armed and ready to play defense for my team should the need arise.

Duke jumped when I sidestepped him so that I could look for her through the window over the grill. "Don't sneak up on a guy."

"Sorry, have you seen Lucille?"

He flipped the sausage patty sputtering in the grease in front of me. "She's flapping her gums out there somewhere."

I stepped up to the cash register at the counter, where I'd have a clear view of most of the tables and found Lucille, making the rounds with a coffee carafe.

Unfortunately, it was Ian Dearborn's cup that she was filling.

He was the last person I needed to be seen with this morning, so I skedaddled back to the relative safety of the kitchen.

"Order up!" Duke gave me an annoyed look as I ducked behind his six-foot-three-inch frame. "What the heck are you doing back there?"

Nothing I wanted to admit to. "Waiting for a bus."

"Uh-huh. Something going on that I should know about?"

"It's girl stuff. Nothing you'd be interested in."

"You got that right," he said, grabbing a couple of eggs while Lucille ambled up to the window.

I waved at her as she reached for the plates under the warming lamp. "I need to talk to you … in private."

Lucille's eyes widened while the little bell over the front door jingled behind her. "What's going on?"

"Girl stuff," Duke answered for me.

"Then this doesn't concern the likes of you," she said, giving him a dirty look. "I'll deliver this order and be right back."

Once Lucille squeaked away, I had a clear view of Steve taking his usual seat at the counter.

Crap.

"Hey, Steve-o," Duke said, giving me a nudge. "Go pour your boyfriend some coffee."

Ordinarily, I'd be happy to keep him supplied with as

much bad coffee as he could stomach. This morning, I wished that he could have waited for Ian to leave before getting here.

Steve smiled at me. "Good morning, sunshine."

Duke aimed his spatula at him. "I've told you not to call me that unless we're alone."

"Sorry, *sweetheart,* I lost my head," Steve dead-panned, holding up an empty cup. "Probably 'cause I haven't had my coffee yet."

My great-uncle turned that spatula on me. "Are you waiting for an engraved invitation?"

"I thought you didn't want the paying customers to feel compelled to help out around here."

"They should be willing to pitch in if they want to keep their family discount," he quipped.

"Fine." A coffee fill-up accompanied by a quick hello. No big deal. Ian was sitting thirty feet away with his back to Steve and looked as though he was engrossed in conversation with some business type at his table.

It should be safe enough. Plus, it wasn't like I had done anything wrong. I just didn't want yesterday's meet-up in the park with Ian to be misinterpreted—especially by Steve.

"Be right there, sir," I said as I walked past him to the coffee station.

"About time you got your sweet butt out here." Steve kept his voice low while I poured java as black as coal tar into his cup. "I was beginning to think you were avoiding me."

"Don't be silly. You're the last person I want to avoid this morning." Truly. Because I could see Ian pushing away from his table, and he'd be heading in this direction any second.

"I should see if Duke or Alice need a refill," I said, inching toward the kitchen.

Before I was able to make a clean getaway, Steve grabbed my hand. "What's the rush?"

I glanced over at Ian, giving me a little wave as he and the man in the suit he'd been sitting with approached the register.

Crikey.

There wasn't a rush anymore.

Setting the coffee carafe next to Steve, I pasted a smile on my face. "Let me ring him up." So that Ian can get out of here. "And then I'll be happy to join you for breakfast."

"Is that Ian Dearborn?" Steve asked.

Unfortunately. "Yep."

"Good morning, Ian." I turned up the wattage of my smile as I reached for his order ticket. "Lucille's a little busy right now, but I'm happy to ring you up."

"Great." He handed me a credit card. "In fact, I'm glad I ran into you."

"Oh?" That made one of us.

"I wanted to thank you again for yesterday."

"No thanks needed." I swiped Ian's card and handed it back to him. "Fozzie loves going to the park."

Locked on my gaze, he leaned in. "Then maybe we can do it again sometime."

Fifteen-year-old me would have melted on the spot upon hearing that Ian Dearborn wanted to see me again. Almost thirty-five-year-old me started to sweat. "I—"

"Maybe next Sunday. Same time?"

"Fozzie would like that," I said, blurting out the first

thing I could think of to get his feet moving toward the door.

Ian grinned. "It's a date, then."

My cheeks burned as I stifled a cringe. "Have a nice day."

Go. Please go.

"Hey, Steve." Ian extended his hand to the observant detective sitting at the counter. "Good to see you again."

"It's been a long time." Steve gave him an easy smile.

Ian shifted his attention to the suit inspecting the fish tank by the door. "I've got somebody waiting for me, but we should get together for a beer some night."

"Any time." Steve reached into a back pocket of his tan chinos and handed Ian a business card. "I'll buy. Just give me a call."

After a final handshake, the door jingled shut behind Ian and the suit, and Steve dropped the smile.

"So, where were we?" I said, sliding onto the vinyl surface of the barstool next to him.

He took a sip of coffee. "I believe you were about to tell me about what you did yesterday."

Something that would have been much easier to explain before Ian and I made a date for next Sunday.

Crap. Crap. Crap.

Chapter Sixteen

"AND YOU JUST made another date with him?" Lucille asked, her hands planted on her round hips as she scowled at me in the middle of the kitchen.

"It's not a date. It's just to let his daughter play with Fozzie."

"He sounds like a guy who needs to get his girl her own dog, or Carmen had it right when she called me last night." Lucille's expression softened. "Ian Dearborn wants to get into your pants."

Good grief. "Don't be ridiculous."

"Order up!" Duke barked.

"Hey, I won't judge if you want to spread your wings." Lucille nudged me with her elbow. "Or any other appendages."

"That's not gonna happen and I'll thank you to not suggest otherwise. Besides, Steve and I are very happy."

"Yeah, he looked real happy," she said, squeaking away to pick up her order.

No, he didn't. Steve had looked disappointed in me, and I didn't blame him. I hadn't been totally honest with him about why I had wanted to see Ian, and Steve knew it.

"What a mess," I muttered, wishing I could have a do-over of this morning.

Aunt Alice glanced up from the flour she was measuring into a mixing bowl. "What's the matter, honey? Are you and Steve having a problem?"

"It's nothing." I hoped.

"This nothing wouldn't have something to do with what Carmen saw in the park, would it?"

"Criminy! Does everyone know about that?"

Alice's cheeks flushed. "I'll have you know that I told that busybody that she had it all wrong. Uh ... she *did* have it all wrong, didn't she?"

"Yes. It's not at all the way it looked."

She squinted at me over her trifocals. "Then you're not seeing Ian Dearborn again."

"I ... um ... not exactly," I said, starting to sweat again.

"Girl, are you telling me that Lucille's right? You're going on another date with him?"

"Jeez Louise! It's not a date!"

Four hours later, I said the same thing to my grandmother after she insisted that I come over for lunch.

"Darn that Carmen and her big mouth," I groaned, burying my head in my hands at Gram's kitchen table. "The only reason Ian asked me to go to the park was so that his daughter could see my dog."

Gram joined me at the table with two tuna sandwiches. "Out of the blue he calls you because he wanted to meet Fozzie."

"Not exactly."

"What's that supposed to mean?"

I stared down at the sandwich I had no appetite for. "He met Fozzie when I took him to get checked out at his clinic."

"Then this actually was a date. Does Steve know?"

"No! I mean yes, he knows. But the only reason I wanted to see Ian was to find out what he knew about Ted's death."

Gram gaped at me. "What he knew? Are you saying that he was there on that trail to see—"

"No, but since he seems to be the one who got his mom to call it off with Mr. Skerrett, I thought I should talk to him."

"Oh, my. History seems to be repeating itself."

I pushed my plate away. "What do you mean by that?"

"Nothing much. That thing with Mitzi that I said I'd tell you about later?"

I nodded, watching Gram take a big bite of her sandwich.

"Of course, this is ancient history," she said with her mouth full. "But I ran into Mitzi at the bank the day after she told Carmen that she was running off to Vegas with Ted to get a quickie divorce."

Whoa. "I'm confused. I heard that Mitzi cleaned out her husband's business account and *then* left town."

"She did, but something happened that must have given Ted a change of heart because I saw with my own eyes that Mitzi didn't get very far."

"When you saw her at the bank."

Gram looked down at her sandwich. "It was pitiful to see her weeping at the counter while she tried to return the money. I remember that I was about to leave but worried about her being able to drive, so I offered her a ride. That's when she lost it."

I hoped that meant that Mitzi opened up to her. "What happened?"

"We sat for a little while. She didn't say much. Seems to me that she mainly just cried—"

"Over him."

"Yep. I guess it was true love...on her part, anyway."

"Did she know what changed his mind?" I asked.

"For one I think he sobered up, but I'm pretty sure that some family intervention was involved."

"Ted's sister, right?"

Gram blinked. "How could you possibly know that?"

I didn't want to get into what I'd overheard. "Lucky guess. What else did Mitzi say?"

"She was crying so hard that it was difficult to understand what she was saying, but I was able to get the gist of it—that Brenda thought Mitzi wasn't good enough for her brother."

Interesting. And would certainly explain the war of words I'd witnessed in the parking lot.

"Maybe it was because we were at the bank, but I remember thinking that it had something to do with money." Gram smiled across the table at me. "Or your granny's old brain is playing tricks on her."

"Your brain's just fine." Because Gram was right. When it came to Ted Skerrett, history had definitely been repeating itself.

✳

After lunch, Patsy sent me north to Port Townsend

to get a statement from one of the witnesses who would be testifying in a property dispute case on the docket for September.

Port Townsend was an artsy community with a vibrant downtown lined with eclectic shops and galleries. Just thirty-two miles away from Gram's house, it served as the destination of convenience for Donna, Rox, and me when we wanted a girls' night out.

I found Port Townsend to be an even more convenient destination today because Ivie Antique Gallery and Appraisals was located across the street from the commercial real estate agent I'd come to interview.

That real estate agent turned out to be the uncooperative witness I'd recently overheard one of the assistant prosecutors complain to Shondra about.

Since the guy had clearly skated on our afternoon appointment, leaving a surly receptionist to provide me a bogus excuse about a sudden emergency, it didn't look like his level of cooperation was about to take a turn for the better.

Whatever.

I was happy to come back tomorrow. I just wouldn't call first. Much like I hadn't called the number on Lawrence Ivie's business card prior to crossing the street and showing up on his doorstep. Sometimes there was no advantage in securing a block of someone's time, especially when that someone wanted to see some collectables I didn't own.

A buzzer sounded when I entered through the heavy door of the brown brick building that housed the Ivie antique store.

The musty-smelling interior resembled the dozen

antique malls my grandmother had dragged me to when she was building her collection of blue Depression glass. Several well-lit display cases sparkled with vintage jewelry near the front windows to attract foot traffic, while shelves stocked with household items from bygone eras edged a path to what could double for a 1930s furniture store complete with an ornate canopy bed.

A smiling woman with a long silver braid stood behind a desk bookended by shelves of mismatched china. She took off her black-framed glasses. "May I help you?"

I waved at the heavy-set man walking in my direction in the same cheap suit that I'd seen him wearing yesterday. "There's the person I'm here to see. Hello, Mr. Ivie."

"Well, hello. This is an unexpected pleasure." Mr. Ivie shifted his attention to the woman. "Grace, this is the young lady I told you about."

She came around the desk and extended her hand. "Grace Ivie. Lawrence's partner in crime."

Only half his size and wearing several strands of glass beads over a flowing violet gauze dress, she looked more like an aging hippie than the woman I'd expect to hear introduce herself as his partner.

"Charmaine Digby. Nice to meet you." I turned back to Mr. Ivie. "And I hope that I'm not here at an inconvenient time, but I need to speak with you for a few minutes."

He furrowed his heavy brow. "You didn't bring your collection here, did you? Because I'm afraid—"

"No, actually this is about another matter. Is there someplace we could talk?"

"Of course," Mr. Ivie said, shooting Grace a wary

sidelong glance. "We can speak in my office."

After he led me past the canopy bed to a cramped back room, he offered me a seat in what appeared to be an orphaned dining room chair opposite his tidy desk.

He eased his girth onto a creaky desk chair and sharpened his gaze on me. "What's this about?"

I flashed him my badge. "The deputy coroner in charge of the Ted Skerrett case asked me to get a statement from everyone who interacted with him on the day he died."

I'd surely lose my badge if Shondra were around to hear those words come out of my mouth, but I had to say something that sounded convincing.

Tucking my badge away, I pulled my notebook from my tote. "I understand that you and another appraiser went to his house that Friday."

Mr. Ivie did the furrowed-brow thing again, looking like a Cro-Magnon man on steroids as he folded his big mitts on the ink blotter in front of him. "Grace and I were contracted to do an appraisal of the estate— something we frequently do as a team when there's a large collection."

"And how did Mr. Skerrett seem to you?"

"Seem?"

"What was his mood?"

"It was the first time I'd met the man, so I would have had no frame of reference to know."

"Uh-huh." *You know plenty.*

"Did you encounter anyone else at the house when you were there?" I asked to find out how forthcoming he'd be regarding the exchange with Marc and Holly.

"Mr. Skerrett's sister was there." Lawrence Ivie's

gaze tightened, his nostrils twitching as if he were taking sudden offense at the musty odor permeating his office. "She seemed rather inclined to hover while we were in the house."

"Anyone else that you spoke with?"

"I believe some other family members arrived just as we were leaving. Grace and I didn't have any real interaction with them."

Even if Holly hadn't given me her account of how the scene played out when she and Marc got out of their car, I would have known Mr. Ivie was lying. Not only by his increased twitching, but by the way he was qualifying his answers. "Was that because of Mr. Skerrett's actions or his sister's?"

He cleared his throat as if to mentally reset himself. "Mr. Skerrett made it quite clear that we were not to discuss the matter of his estate with anyone else. Not that we would. We have a contractual obligation to respect our clients' privacy."

"I'm sure you do," I said, jotting a note about the contract. When I looked up, I noticed that Mr. Ivie seemed to be shrinking in his oversize worsted wool.

"If Ms. Proctor has said otherwise ..." He pressed his fleshy lips together as if his mouth needed a timeout. "I assure you that it's not the case."

I knew what he wanted to hear—an assurance from me about whatever dealings he now had with Brenda.

Mr. Ivie wasn't going to get it that easily. "She does have some rather strong opinions regarding the estate."

"Indeed," he said, squeezing his hands together so tight his knuckles were white.

"I assume that Brenda Proctor is now your client?"

"Not as yet."

That wasn't the answer I had expected to hear. "I thought I understood you to say that you had a contract to appraise the estate."

"We did, with Mr. Skerrett."

"And that contract was..." I didn't know enough about how contracts worked to ask a decent question.

"Fulfilled."

"Your work was completed?"

"We had to do some research to complete our report, but we mailed it to Mr. Skerrett last Monday."

"After his death, so he never found out the value of his estate."

Pulling out a handkerchief, Mr. Ivie took a swipe at the beads of sweat peppering his upper lip. "Estimated value, but correct."

Then why had Ted thrown himself between the appraisers and Holly like a human shield? "Mr. Skerrett must have suspected that there were some items of great value in the house. Otherwise, he probably wouldn't have arranged for your services."

"That's typical in these situations."

As in *duh*. "How much money are we talking?"

He straightened. "*We* are not talking about any matters specific to the appraisal."

Dang. "But Ms. Proctor and you have been in some discussion about it." I referred back to my notes. "Although you said she wasn't your client *yet*."

Mr. Ivie ran his handkerchief over his drippy brow. "We're in negotiation."

"Negotiation" isn't the word I would have used to describe the exchange I heard yesterday afternoon. "I see. But since the appraisal has already been completed, what are you negotiating about?"

"That's a private matter that has nothing to do with what happened to her brother," he said, his volume increasing as he slapped his palms to the edge of his desk and pushed to his feet. "Now, if you'll excuse me, I have work I need to get back to."

"Of course. Just one more question. When I asked you about establishing a value for some Civil War items in my possession, you asked if I wanted to sell them."

He stood by his door like an overdressed bouncer, itching to toss me from the room. "That's what most of our clients want to do when they're in *actual* possession of something they have little or no emotional attachment to."

Okay, so I lied. It got me another step closer to understanding what was going on with Ted Skerrett that Friday, and I wasn't about to offer any apologies for that.

I closed the distance between us to get a better view of Lawrence Ivie's face. "So you find other collectors who would be interested in what your client has to sell?"

He tucked in his double chin as he scowled down at me. "We're not matchmakers. There are regional estate sales if we decide to not sell on consignment." He gave his head a little shake as if he'd just censored himself. "The venue depends on the value and rarity of the item."

"I'm sure it does."

Just as I was sure that was why Brenda wasn't letting Holly in to remove any of those dolls. At least one of them had to be worth a small fortune.

Chapter Seventeen

THE FIRST THING I did when I got back to the courthouse was to tell Assistant Prosecutor Lisa Arbuckle that the witness for her upcoming case had been a no-show.

After assuring the petite blonde fuming in the pin-striped pantsuit that I'd get the guy's statement before the week was out, I figured I might have bought myself enough goodwill to ask her legal opinion about what I had gleaned from my unofficial interview.

Without mentioning any specifics that could get me into deep doodoo with Shondra, I told Lisa that a friend of mine was having a problem with the executor of her mother's will.

Before I got thirty seconds into my story, Lisa raised her hand to cut me off. "Tell your friend to get a lawyer, because she's definitely got a case."

"What kind of case?" I asked.

"You say the executor is intentionally depriving your friend of her property?"

"That's pretty much how she described the situation to me."

"That's fraud."

"Whoa." Maybe the small fortune that Brenda had been protecting wasn't so small.

"Don't sound so surprised. Greed's a powerful motivator."

Way too true, but what could some vintage dolls be worth?

Certainly they had value enough for Lawrence Ivie to fight for the commission on their sale. But was it worth the cost of a man's life?

With Lisa focused on the laptop in front of her, I opened my mouth to thank her, but she shooed me toward her door as the cell phone in my tote started to buzz. "She needs to talk to a lawyer, but this sounds like a case for probate court."

"Right." I wasn't sure how I could relay that advice to Holly without getting more involved in this non-case than I already was, but I couldn't sit on this knowledge and do nothing. "Thanks," I said, stepping into the hallway to answer my phone.

"Where the heck have you been?" Donna demanded, raising her voice over some mewling background noise. "I've been trying to reach you for hours."

This didn't sound like it was going to be a short conversation, so I ducked into an empty conference room and shut the door. "Working. What's going on?"

"That's what we want to know."

"*We?*"

"Oh, honey," Donna said. "You really need to check your messages more often. Just tell me that you're coming."

"Where? What are you talking about?"

"Check your darn messages, and get your hiney over

to Roxie's. We'll be waiting for you."

"But—"

I looked down at my phone. Not only had my call ended, I'd missed two others and had five text messages —all from Donna. Not one of them explained why she had called some sort of emergency meeting at Rox's house.

But I could venture a guess: Carmen.

Ten minutes after I left the office, Rox greeted me at her front door with a warm hug and an easy grin. "Guess who heard some news about you today," she said over the frenetic yapping coming from her living room.

Since Donatello's, Donna's beauty salon, was Gossip South to Duke's Gossip Central, I cringed to think of the wagging tongues that would have sat in her chair today. But I couldn't help but wonder if something else was wagging in the next room. "Did you and Eddie get a dog?"

"No, but wait until you see who did. Want a glass of the wine Donna brought over?"

"Sure." I had a feeling I'd be in need of a drink.

While Rox headed into the kitchen, I peeked around the corner and found Donna smiling up at me from the sofa with a tiny, yappy dog on her lap.

"You got a dog?" I asked, sitting on the cushion next to her.

Donna fingered the ruby red bow at the base of the dog's curly topknot. "It's temporary. Gladys is having gallbladder surgery tomorrow, and I'm taking care of Pumpkin for the next couple of weeks."

Gladys was one of the ladies in my grandmother's mahjong group, and she lived on the other side of town from Donna's apartment, so it wasn't like the dog-sitting offer had been extended because she was being a good neighbor. "That's very nice of you."

"I know," she said, fluffing Pumpkin's topknot as the little dog settled down and stretched out a pink tongue to lick Donna's hand. "And see? We're already good friends."

"This sudden friendship wouldn't have anything to do with Ian Dearborn, would it?"

Donna lifted her perfectly arched brows. "Excuse me. After what you've been up to, you've got a lot of nerve to suggest—"

"I'm not up to anything." Much.

"Oh, sure. Using your dog so that you could hook up with Ian."

I looked up at the amused pregnant lady delivering my wine. "I didn't. That appointment at his clinic was strictly for business purposes."

"Business?" Rox asked, settling into the swivel rocker opposite the sofa.

Maybe I should have used a less descriptively accurate adjective. "I just mean that it wasn't anything beyond a doctor/patient visit."

Donna's glossy lips curled into a humorless smile. "How about the visit where you were seen holding his hand at the park?"

Egads. "I see Carmen made it to your shop today."

Donna ran her hand down the silvery back of the little dog on her lap. "I'm not divulging my source. We'll just call the person a reliable eyewitness."

I set my wineglass down on the coffee table before I snapped off the stem. "Believe me when I tell you that Carmen's not *that* reliable in this case."

"So you deny holding his hand?" Donna asked.

I exchanged glances with Rox. "Really, it's not the way it looked."

Donna huffed a breath. "I can't believe that you'd use your dog to make a move on Ian."

"That's not what I was doing." But I had no desire to admit that I had suspected Ian might be capable of murder, so it was time to turn the tables on her.

I pointed at the ball of fluff curled on her lap. "Unlike what you were planning to do with this little girl."

Donna jutted her chin at me. "I'll have you know that I'm doing Gladys a favor because if I didn't volunteer, she was going to have to board Pumpkin and cancel—"

"Her appointment with Ian?" I said with a smile.

She smacked her lips with annoyance. "I'm still doing her a favor, but I won't take it any further than that if you're really interested in him."

"I'm not." At least not in the way she meant.

Rox rocked back and forth. "See, Donna? I told you."

Donna shifted her attention back to me. "Then you don't have another date with him."

"It's not a real date. It's a play date between Fozzie and Peyton." Which gave me an idea that would nip my *date* problem in the bud. "In fact, are you working Sunday afternoon?"

Donna shook her head.

"Then you and Pumpkin should join us at the park. I'll even take Fozzie on a walk with Peyton so that you can be alone with her dad."

Donna's sapphire eyes gleamed with interest. "Won't that seem too much like a setup?"

Rox chuckled as she rested her bare feet on the coffee table separating us. "After practically kidnapping that oversized rat on your lap, do you really care?"

"Don't listen to your aunt Roxie, Pumpkin," Donna cooed, placing her hands over the dog's pointy ears. "She's just bitter because she has swollen ankles."

I didn't like the sound of that. "Rox, are you okay?"

"I'm fine. I just need to put my feet up more often." She ran her palm over her belly. "Of course, I'd feel even better if Junior wouldn't kick his mama every time I sit down."

Donna handed Pumpkin to me and pushed off the sofa. "Is he doing that now?" she asked, staring at Rox's protruding tummy as if an alien life form could burst out at any second.

Rox guided Donna's hand. "Wait for it."

No one moved, not even Pumpkin.

After a few seconds, Donna beamed. "Well, I know what I'm getting this kid for his first birthday. A soccer ball."

Leaving Pumpkin on the sofa so that I could get in on this action, I placed my palm on Rox's belly. I didn't have to wait long to feel the baby move. "Wow."

"I know," Donna said, wiping a tear from her eye. "Doesn't it make you want one?"

Yes. "No, but Auntie Char will be happy to borrow this one anytime you need a babysitter."

Rox yawned.

Between working full time and growing her little soccer player, she was obviously sleep-deprived. "Or a nap."

Closing her eyes, she patted my hand. "Deal."

"In the meantime..." I turned to Donna. "How about it? Would you and Pumpkin care to join me and Fozzie at the park Sunday?"

Donna picked up the tiny dog and hugged her. "We'd love to!"

One little problem down, one very big one to go.

Chapter Eighteen

IT WAS CLOSE to six-thirty when I left Rox's house. I figured that should be late enough for Holly and Marc to be home from work, making it high time for someone in this big, fat mess to clue them in on the value of their mother's estate.

I just wished that someone didn't have to be me, especially since I didn't want it getting back to Frankie or Shondra that I was poking around the fringes of a non-active death investigation.

So, when my call to Holly went to voice mail, I felt some relief that the savvier of the two siblings wasn't available to ask me why I was recommending that she find an attorney to advocate on her behalf.

Holly was smart. She could figure it out.

Same with her brother when I left a similar message.

A good attorney should be able to get them a hearing where they could fight for what was rightfully theirs. Beyond the suggestion I was offering, I wanted nothing to do with this pissing match over Ruth Skerrett's estate. Although I couldn't help but suspect that Ted's death was somehow connected to it.

If it wasn't, Ted falling to his death hours after the

discovery of some treasure in his house seemed like the freakiest of coincidences. And as Shondra had told me on more than one occasion, she wasn't a big believer in coincidences.

Neither am I, but when I pulled into the Red Apple parking lot a few minutes later and saw Nate Falco exiting the store, I was grateful for a bit of lucky timing.

"Hey, Nate," I said, scrambling out of my car and into the drizzly mist blowing in from Merritt Bay. "Fancy meeting you here."

With his face shielded by the bill of his red Falco Charters ball cap, Nate was difficult to read, but he hadn't reached for the handle of his faded black pickup, so I took that as another good sign.

"I keep running into you," he muttered, making it clear that only one of us viewed this as a positive thing.

"I know, and it's fortunate timing, because I wanted to ask how your mom was doing."

Nate's gaze tightened. "She's fine. Went home right after the funeral."

"I ask because I hadn't expected to see her there, not after that exchange with Ted's sister."

"Yeah, well, I'm pretty sure my mother was there for him, not her."

Transferring the weight of the sack of groceries in his arms, Nate took a step toward his door—an obvious cue that my luck was about to run out.

"Nate, you said something about giving Ted the invitation. I know it's none of my business, but were you and Andy trying to make peace with Ted? Maybe as part of the reconciliation you've had with your mom?" That Andy had once talked to me about, when their mother tried to make amends after years of estrangement.

Nate stared into the mist, his mouth set in a grim line. "Just me. I just wanted all the old crap between our families to be over and done with."

I wasn't completely following. "So you invited him to your brother's wedding."

"Seemed like a good idea at the time." Nate opened the driver's side door and set his groceries on the passenger seat. "Then Ted went and got himself killed before he could apologize to her for everything that happened back then."

My pulse pounded in my ears like an alarm going off. "Excuse me?"

"I really thought he'd changed. My mom certainly had, with the help of a lot of AA meetings. But after what Brenda said to her in that parking lot ..." Nate pulled his ball cap down over his furrowed brow as he slid behind the wheel. "I don't think that anymore."

With everything I'd learned about Ted Skerrett in the last week, I wouldn't think that either.

After I got my groceries home and fed Fozzie, I took a page out of Donna's playbook and called Aunt Alice to meet me at Gram's for an emergency family meeting.

"The game's on so this'd better be good," Duke groused at me twenty minutes later, when I greeted him and Alice at Gram's front door. "'Cause if it's about your mother's wedding, we're outta here."

"It's not, but I need your wife more than you, so if you want to watch the game ..." I pointed at the remote on the living room coffee table. "Go for it."

He shoved his rain-spotted jacket into my hands. "At least let me hear what the emergency's about before you try to get rid of me."

Alice took a last glance across the street at Steve's dimly lit house before I shut the door. "You're not going to tell us that you broke up over that business with Ian Dearborn, are you?"

"No!" I could hardly believe my ears that we were still talking about that stupid *business*.

I grabbed a couple of hangers from the closet for their coats. "But it does have something to do with Ian's mother."

"Not this again," Duke grumbled.

"Yes, this again." And then some.

I escorted them into the dining room, where my grandmother was waiting with a fresh pot of decaf to accompany the store-bought strawberry cheesecake she'd started thawing when I called to say that we were coming.

When I slipped into the chair next to Gram, she gave me a parental glare. "Charmaine Marie Digby, you had me worried sick. I thought you were going to tell us that your mother's wedding was off."

I wish.

Picking up the carafe, I filled our two cups. "No, I want you to explain why people keep telling me that they think Ted Skerrett did something to get himself killed."

Scowling, Duke waggled his dessert fork at me. "Probably because somebody keeps poking her nose where it doesn't belong."

I stuck my tongue out at the old coot. "I'll have you know that the more I poke, the more I don't like what

I'm finding out."

"You don't mean that old news about Mitzi," Gram said.

I shook my head. "No, it's newer news."

Alice waved me away when I came around the table to offer her some decaf. "Not the rich widow connection again."

"The what?" Gram asked.

Alice met her sister's gaze. "It's a little theory Lucille and I came up with because of what Winnie and Ruth had in common."

Wide-eyed, Gram sucked in a breath. "Money."

"And some desirable property," I added. "Which Ted apparently ended up leaving to Brenda, pretty much screwing Ruth's children out of their inheritance."

Gram's fork clanged to her plate. "You're not suggesting that Holly or Marc—"

"I'm not suggesting anything other than the fact that Ted Skerrett might've screwed a few other people over the years."

Duke smirked. "Mitzi certainly comes to mind."

"I wasn't talking about that kind of screwing, you dirty old man," I said, reaching for my cup to wash away that mental image. "Have you heard any rumors about the guy ticking someone else off?"

Duke turned to his wife. "Rumors are more your department."

Alice heaved a sigh. "I beg your pardon. I just like to keep up with current events."

I didn't care what Alice called it. I just wanted to know everything she'd heard. "And?"

"Other than hearing that Ian wasn't too keen about

Winnie getting involved with Ted, I got nothing."

"What about back when Ted married Ruth?" I asked. "Given what you all knew about him, didn't their getting together seem a little suspicious at the time?"

"Honey, that was such a long time ago, and I barely knew Ruth back then. It wasn't until she hooked up with Nadine and Winnie and joined the Gray Ladies that I spent any real time with her." Alice looked at my grandmother. "When was that? Maybe fifteen years ago?"

Gram nodded. "I'd known her through the garden club back when Jerry was still alive. The Library Guild, too. In fact, I think it was at a Guild luncheon that Ruth announced her engagement to Ted."

"You had to have been surprised after everything you'd heard about him from Mitzi, right?" I asked.

A crease carved a path between Gram's brows. "A little at first. But Ruthie seemed so happy, I think I wanted to believe that Ted had changed."

That seemed to be a common refrain tonight.

"Ruthie never seemed to have one unkind thing to say about him," Gram added.

Duke scoffed. "Then love really is blind."

I stared across the table at him. "What do you know?"

He shrugged. "You saw how he was."

"A pretty shameless flirt." At least with me.

"Yeah," Duke said as if he had a bad taste in his mouth.

Gram gaped at her brother-in-law. "Are you trying to imply that he was cheating on Ruth?"

Duke forked another bite of cheesecake. "I'm just

sayin' that the guy had an eye for the ladies. *All* of the ladies."

"If he were cheating with one of those ladies, don't you think we would've heard?" Alice chimed in.

Her husband grunted. "Not everyone blabs as much as you do."

Alice gave him an icy glare. "I'm simply trying to remind you that it's tough to keep a secret around here."

True, but since we were talking about Ted Skerrett, I hoped it wasn't entirely impossible.

Gram looked at me over the rim of her cup. "Sweetheart, I'm sure it's occurred to you that maybe the reason there hasn't been any gossip about Ted—at least prior to him looking for wife number three—is that there isn't any to tell."

Wait a minute. "Wife number *three*? He was married before Ruth?"

"It's one of the many things she had in common with him," Gram said. "They were both recently widowed."

"I had no idea." But I sure wondered how that fit into the rich widow theory.

"I'm sure there's a lot that we'll never know about the man, including how he ended up in that ravine." Gram patted my hand. "So maybe it's time to accept that fact and let this go."

With everything I'd found out in the last week? Not a chance.

While I squeezed out a smile, the back door creaked open and I craned my neck to see a dejected-looking Marietta enter the kitchen.

"Oh, Mary Jo," Gram said, looking back over her shoulder. "I didn't expect you home this early."

"There's been a change of plans." Marietta burst into tears as she stepped into the dining room. "Because ... of the ... weather."

The weather? I peered out at the rain spattering the glass slider door that opened to the back deck. "It's not raining that hard."

My mother buried her face in her hands. "You don't understand."

There were lots of things I didn't understand about her. And I wasn't sure that I cared to understand how a few sprinkles could ruin her evening.

Gram pushed her chair back and wrapped Marietta in her arms. "Good heavens, sweetheart. What's wrong?"

"I have to cancel the wedding."

Chapter Nineteen

WHEN STEVE OPENED his front door, he didn't look happy to see the tin of leftover cheesecake in my hands. "What's the occasion?"

"You don't want to know." And I didn't want to tell him.

Duke honked at us as he pulled out of Gram's driveway, and Alice rolled down her window to wave goodbye.

"The game's on," Steve said, tracking their taillights. "Something important must have been going on over there to separate the old man from his TV."

Since there was a high probability of a hungry detective showing up tomorrow for a meal prepared by that old man, I knew that I had better offer up a plausible explanation. "I—"

Steve muttered an obscenity, shutting the door behind me. "Don't tell me that I forgot your birthday."

Huh?

I'd been so busy I hadn't given my upcoming birthday a thought. "No, that's Thursday. The cheesecake was Gram's idea when I called a family meeting."

Following me to his kitchen, he blew out a breath.

"Now what has your mother done?"

Since talking about Marietta was a safer subject than Ted Skerrett, I was happy to deliver the latest news. "She's cancelled the wedding."

Steve opened his refrigerator and offered up a long-necked bottle of beer. "Are we celebrating or commiserating?"

"Neither, but I'll have a sip of yours."

"One sip," he said as if he were making a point of clarification during a negotiation.

"Maybe two."

"Forget it." He pulled out a second bottle. "You're getting your own."

"What's your problem with a little bit of sharing?"

"I have no problem. I just think our definitions of what 'little bit' means are different."

"You can be a real jerk sometimes."

A corner of Steve's mouth quirked into a hint of a smirk. "I know you."

"Then you know I'm happy to share this cheesecake with you."

"Because it's chick food you and your granny are trying to get rid of."

So neither one of us was a woman of mystery.

I set the tin at the center of his kitchen table and took a seat in my usual chair. "If you don't want it, don't eat it."

"Are you gonna tell me why the wedding's off?" he asked, pulling a fork from the silverware drawer.

"It's raining."

Steve dropped into the adjacent chair and handed me one of the bottles. "So?"

"So, it's an outdoor wedding and she's freaked out about it because it's been raining all week."

"Pretty sure that's why you two made sure that they had a big white tent when you booked the place."

I leveled my gaze at him while he stabbed a strawberry. "Does my mother look like someone who wants to get married under the big top?"

"I assume that's a rhetorical question."

"Yeah." I twisted off the bottle cap and took a swig.

"What's Barry have to say about this?"

I stole Steve's fork and scooped up a strawberry-coated bite. "I'm not sure he knows."

Steve didn't say anything, and I looked up to see him staring at me. "What?" I said with my mouth full.

The laugh lines surrounding his eyes crinkled as if he had an opinion on the matter.

And I was pretty sure I wouldn't enjoy hearing it. "Hey, I'm not going to be the one to tell him."

"I didn't say you were." He took back his fork. "It just occurred to me that you might be off your diet."

I shrugged. "If there isn't going to be a wedding, I can have a couple of extra strawberries." With a little cheesecake attached.

His eyes darkened as they zeroed in on my lips. "Maybe you'd like to share."

My heart fluttered at the prospect that he wanted to taste more than just a strawberry. "I thought that's what we were doing."

"Well, there's sharing." Putting the fork down, Steve pressed his lips to mine, taking his time as he deepened the kiss. "And then there's sharing."

I couldn't help but smile as I wrapped my arms

around his neck. "I do like it when you share."

"I have something else I'd like to share with you."

I glanced down at the bulge straining his zipper. "Do you now."

"Assuming you're still in a sharing mood."

"What'd you have in mind?"

Grinning, Steve pulled me to my feet. "You know exactly what I have in mind."

"I believe I do," I managed to utter a split second before he plundered my mouth.

Holy smokes, I felt like I was dissolving into a puddle of strawberry cream.

While I buzzed with electricity.

Steve ran his fingers over the hip pocket of my jeans. "Your butt is buzzing."

I didn't care. "It's just a text." I flattened my breasts against his chest to pick up where we'd left off. "It can wait."

"Good. Now, where were we?" he asked, tightening his embrace as he reclaimed my lips.

And that's when my phone started ringing.

Give me a break, Mom!

Steve pulled my phone from my pocket and handed it to me. "Maybe you should take this one."

Because he knew as well as I did that my mother would keep calling. Worse, end up on his doorstep if she looked outside and saw my car. "Fine."

But it wasn't Marietta's name displayed on the screen of my cell phone, it was Gram's.

Uh-oh. My grandmother never called unless something was wrong.

"What's up?" I asked, stepping into Steve's living

room so that I could look out his front window.

"I'm sorry to bother you, but I saw your car outside." Gram's voice trembled with a sense of urgency, as if she were having trouble breathing. "Could you come over for a few minutes? I need your help."

I raced toward the door. "Are you okay?"

"I'm fine. It's your mother."

It was quiet when I opened my grandmother's front door. Too quiet, considering the phone call I had just received.

Following the soft glow of the light over the stove, I rounded the corner and spotted Gram and my mother sitting at the kitchen table.

Both had a glass of wine in front of them. The stem of Marietta's glass was obscured by a sea of used tissues. Judging by the dark smears on them, my mother hadn't opted to wear her waterproof mascara today. But the wine appeared untouched.

"Is this a private wine-tasting, or can anybody join in?" I asked, locking gazes with Gram.

She pushed her glass toward me as I took the seat next to her. "We can share."

Since I had anticipated sharing something entirely different right about now, I slapped a smile on my face. "So what are you girls talking about?" As if I didn't know.

Marietta blew her nose and then let the tissue tumble down to the table. "We're done talking."

"We most certainly are not," Gram stated in her most authoritative voice.

My mother gave me a pained look. "Is it still raining out?"

My damp hair was frizzing before her bloodshot eyes, so there was no point in denying it. "A little."

"Just like last night and the night before that." Tears cut a path down Marietta's pale cheeks. "If it keeps up, Rainshadow Ridge will probably flood. Not only will the wedding be cancelled, everyone in the area will have to evacuate."

Gram heaved a sigh as she handed her daughter another tissue. "The venue is called *Rainshadow* Ridge Resort for a reason."

Marietta dabbed her eyes. "I don't care what it's called, I spoke to the manager and it was raining there two hours ago."

"Did he tell you what the forecast is for Saturday?" I asked.

She sniffed. "No."

"Then let's take a look." I pulled out my phone and opened up the weather app. "Port Merritt." There was a chance of showers all week, but it was supposed to improve with sunshine predicted for Sunday. And if it was going to be nice here, it would be even better on the Ridge. With any luck, starting Saturday evening.

"I don't think you have anything to worry about." Placing my finger over the day, I held up the screen so that she could see that sunny image. "See?"

Marietta squinted at my phone. "Is that a sun?"

"Yep." I read her the forecast for the weekend, skipping the decreasing chance of showers part. "Maybe you shouldn't be so quick to cancel."

"Do you really think it's going to be okay?" she asked

in a small voice, sounding like a child afraid of the dark.

Gram huffed. "I think everything will be fine if you'll stop acting like a ..." She turned to me. "What do you call her?"

Way to put me on the spot, Gram! "I don't know what you mean."

She pursed her lips. "Sure you do. A drama something."

"A drama queen?" Marietta exclaimed, her puffy eyes narrowing.

Gram pointed at her. "Bingo. Don't be such a drama queen."

My mother tucked in her chin and made a pouty face. "I hate that term."

Pushing up from the table, Gram kissed her daughter's cheek. "Then don't act like one and you won't hear it."

The second Gram stepped away, Marietta glowered at me. "Really? You call me that in front of my own mother?"

"I think we're done here," I announced, getting to my feet.

"No, we're not." She wagged a tapered nail at me. "Sit."

"Steve's waiting for me."

"He won't mind waiting a few more minutes."

Maybe not, but I did. Especially since I had a feeling that the topic of conversation was about to change to something I really didn't want to discuss.

Plopping my butt back down, I exchanged glances with my grandmother when she returned to the table with the wine bottle.

"In case you need reinforcements." Gram planted a kiss on the top of my head. "On that happy note, I'm going upstairs. My show's on."

I seriously doubted my grandmother had a particular TV show she wanted to watch in her room. She'd just had enough downstairs drama for one night. And I couldn't say I blamed her because I felt the same exact way.

The second the stairs creaked under Gram's weight, Marietta leaned forward in her chair. "You don't think I'm making a horrible mistake, do you?"

Since when did my mother care what I thought about her life choices?

I shrugged. "I seriously doubt you'll be saying your *I dos* in a tent, if that's what you're worried about."

She stared down at her untouched wineglass. "I meant getting married again."

Criminy. I wasn't just being put on the spot. I was being pushed onto a trap door.

"It's a big decision," I said, trying to tap dance my way toward safer ground.

Marietta nodded, her eyes glistening with a fresh round of tears. "It is. But lately, with all the rain and the fight we got into over the house, it feels like this marriage isn't getting off to a good start. And I couldn't bear it if this one ..." Emotion clogging her throat, she reached for another tissue.

I hadn't heard anything about a fight, but since my mother had made it sound like the decision to upgrade their future home had been a unilateral one, I could understand if any tempers flared.

I also understood her need to make this relationship

work after the disasters in her past. It was one of the few things that she and I had in common.

But that didn't mean that I could offer her anything beyond a sympathetic ear. "Maybe I'm not the one you should be talking to tonight."

Marietta wiped her eyes. "You mean Barry."

"He's your partner in this." Not me.

"I can't. He'll think I don't want to marry him." Her lips trembled. "It's bad enough that he's barely touched me since I signed the papers on the new house, I can't tell him..."

More than enough said. "If you are unsure about your feelings for him—"

"I'm not! I love him. More than anything. Look at what I've given up so that we can be together. Doesn't that say something?"

It sure did to me.

Marietta Moreau was scared that she hadn't just given up her Malibu home; she was walking away from her career.

It wasn't in my best interest to remind my mother that there was a reason she had fallen off the Hollywood B-list. Because when your biggest claim to fame is filling out a bikini on a southern-fried *Charlie's Angels* ripoff, your agent can have a tough time selling you when you're a menopausal fifty-six-year-old.

"It says a lot." Truly. But that didn't mean she should have been so quick to say yes when Mr. Ferris proposed.

I tried to think of some advice I could leave her with so that I could get back across the street to the safety of Steve's arms. "I still think you should talk to him. If you have any doubts at all..."

Marietta buried her face in her hands and sobbed.

Crap.

I sent Steve a text that I'd see him tomorrow and refilled my wineglass.

Chapter Twenty

"WHAT'S THE LATEST?" Lucille asked, sliding a mug of coffee in front of me as I sat next to Stanley at the counter.

When I tucked my mother in around midnight, she had yet to tell her fiancé that the wedding was off, so I wasn't about to make her Gossip Central's leading news story. "Good morning to you, too."

She waved me off. "Yeah, yeah. I know about that meeting last night at your granny's house, so something's obviously up."

I took that to mean that Lucille hadn't managed to pry any details out of my great-aunt Alice.

Good. Maybe what happened at Gram's could stay at Gram's.

"What's up? Let me think," I said, grabbing a couple of creamers from the dish in front of Stanley. "Gladys is having gallbladder surgery today and Donna's taking care of her dog."

Stanley set his newspaper down on the counter. "Hardly seems like meeting material. Is that the best you can do?"

I flashed him an innocent smile. "It's all I got."

He and Lucille exchanged looks. "I seriously doubt that," she grumbled, frowning at me. "What about the little matter we were looking into on Sunday?"

With everything that had been going on the last couple of days, she needed to narrow her line of questioning. "Which little matter would that be?"

"What do you think? The other woman you-know-who was having that fight with."

"You mean Mitzi?" Stanley asked.

Lucille leaned on the counter in front of him. "What do you know about it?"

He shrugged. "Same as everyone else around here—that there was a cat fight at Andy's wedding."

"Order up," Duke bellowed, glaring at Lucille.

Ignoring the cue to get back to work, she leaned closer. "Any idea who the other cat was?"

Stanley took a loud slurp of decaf. "Thought it must be some distant relative showing up uninvited. You know, some bad blood boiling over in the parking lot."

Stanley had no idea how close to the truth he was. He just had the wrong, not-so-distant family member. "I'm sure that must've been it," I said, hoping that could be the last word on this subject.

"Bad blood boiling over." Lucille squeaked away to pick up her order. "Sounds like someone's been watching too many cop shows."

She was one to talk.

Lucille looked back over her shoulder at me. "You know what you want?"

Yep, bacon and eggs with a side of pancakes, but after last night's cheesecake my hips didn't need an injection of more fat calories. "Egg white omelet, dry wheat toast."

"Two of those," Steve said, giving my damp ponytail a little tug as he sat down beside me.

Wishing I had made more of an effort in front of the mirror prior to accepting Steve's invitation to join him for breakfast, I smiled at him. "Good morning."

He reached for my cup and took a swallow.

"Hey, if you'd wait two seconds, you can have your own cup, you know."

"I thought you wanted to *share*."

"Not everything."

"I see. So it's only when I have something that you want."

I sighed with the knowledge that this was an argument I couldn't win, and reclaimed my cup.

"Good one," Stanley said, extending his fist to Steve, who bumped it in front of my nose.

"Would you two like to be alone?" I asked.

Steve grinned. "You just can't handle the truth."

I took a sip of coffee. "Says you."

Stanley chuckled. "I think he's got you there."

And I thought it was time to move to a booth, where we wouldn't have so much audience participation.

Grabbing my cup, I crooked my finger for Steve to follow me.

"Want me all to yourself, huh?" he said loud enough to turn the heads of Carmen, Nadine, and the other Gray Ladies as they stepped through the front door.

I forced a smile. *Nothing to see here.*

Crossing to the opposite corner, I slid onto the cracked vinyl bench seat. "I thought it would be nice to have a little more privacy." Especially now that Carmen was in the cafe.

"Okay by me, because I wanted to ask how it went last night with your mom," Steve said while Lucille rushed toward us with a steaming coffee carafe.

She angled a glance at me while she took her time filling the cup in front of Steve. "Don't let me interrupt you."

I held out my cup for a refill. "Not a problem. We can wait."

Lucille wrinkled her nose. "You're no fun."

"I would tell her otherwise," Steve said when Lucille squeaked away. "But since you never came back last night..."

"I couldn't leave my mom."

"So she's serious. The wedding's cancelled." He pointed at the droplets dotting the window. "Because of a little bit of rain."

"It's more than that. I think she's finally realized that she said 'yes' before she thought things through."

Steve stirred creamer into his coffee. "Things that would include selling her house and moving a thousand miles north."

"She didn't put it exactly like that, but it seems like it's finally sinking in how much her life will be changing."

"If that's the case, I guess you won't have Barry's house to move into."

"I don't think he was ever that crazy about the idea, anyway. He was just going along with it because my mother hates where I'm living."

Instead of responding, Steve took a sip of coffee.

"It's no big loss." Other than the free rent and the

fenced yard for Fozzie. Plus, the privacy and the great neighborhood with the dog park just four blocks away.

Okay, it might be a bigger loss than I was letting on. "And it would have been way too complicated."

"Because Barry and your mother would have been your landlords."

I nodded.

"What if I had another house I could offer you?"

"Do you have a rental house that I don't know about?"

"I'm talking about my place."

Staring across the table at him, I felt all the air leave my body. "Are you going somewhere?"

Please say you're not leaving me.

The corners of his lips lifted. "No, you'd have to share the house with me, but considering how much you like *sharing*, I thought you might not mind."

Steve and I had never talked about living together before.

In fact, we'd never had a serious conversation about our relationship since the August night he took me to bed, obliterating the rules that had governed our friendship.

There had been no exchange of "I love yous." At least I hadn't blurted anything out loud. But what we'd had all these months was entirely sufficient. Heck, it had been beyond anything I could have imagined, but I had to remain realistic and accept our relationship for what it was: We were sex buddies.

Not that I was complaining.

It had been great to feel desired again, and this time by a guy I completely trusted. A best friend.

Who lived right across the street from my grand-mother.

I knew she couldn't love Steve more if he were her own grandson, and had never once mentioned the "M" word around me. Probably because she didn't want me to make the same mistake as her daughter and rush into another marriage.

But I had moved out of Gram's house for an important reason: so that if this sex-buddy thing went south, I wouldn't make the situation more complicated for my grandmother than it already was.

I swallowed the lump growing in my throat. "I appreciate the offer. I really do, but I think it's best if we don't live together right now."

Steve fixed me with a piercing gaze. "What's 'right now' supposed to mean?"

"That I think it's important for me to live on my own for a while."

"Okay," he muttered as if it were anything but.

"Doesn't mean there can't be sleepovers, though," I added with a smile, hoping to lighten the mood.

"Uh-huh." Steve's cell phone rang and he scowled at the caller ID on the display. "Sorry, I need to take this."

"No problem." But I wished he didn't, because I clearly needed to make Steve understand why I wasn't jumping at the chance to share his bed every night.

He headed toward the door. "Hey, Captain."

When the silver bell jingled behind him, I noticed Lucille coming over with our breakfast order.

"Steve's not leaving, is he?" she asked, setting down the plates.

I didn't hear any sirens in the distance, so I doubted

that Port Merritt's detective division was going to have to skip the breakfast she had ready for him. "I don't think so."

Flattening her palms on the table, Lucille lowered her voice. "You two didn't have a fight, did you?"

"No. We were just talking."

"Obviously about something serious. Having to do with your mom?"

Jeez, leave it alone, Lucille. "Having to do with something that's none of your business."

Her mouth pulled into a tight grimace as she straightened. "No fun whatsoever. That's what you've become."

The pit in my stomach told me that Steve would soon be echoing that sentiment.

A half hour after Steve wolfed down his omelet and lied about a meeting he had to run off to, I drove to the courthouse welcoming eight hours where no one would want to talk to me about weddings, my relationship with Steve, or my seedy apartment.

With Patsy out running an errand for Frankie, I'd even managed to avoid my morning ration of snark, and considered it a bonus to have a blessed few quiet moments alone with a gurgling coffee pot while I tidied up the breakroom. But before I had a chance to wash the cups someone had left in the sink, Lisa Arbuckle marched up in a pair of loud, chunky heels.

"What the heck are you doing?" she demanded, her hands planted on her slim hips.

"My job." What did it look like?

Her jaw clenched. "Did you not get my message?"

Well, this little day just kept getting better and better. "I haven't been to my desk yet. What's going on?"

"One of the witnesses in my land dispute case just called to report that Grant Sweezy was pressuring her to change her story."

Which helped explain why the commercial real estate agent ducked out of his interview with me yesterday.

I was no legal expert, but even I understood that Mr. Sweezy could damage Lisa's case if someone didn't reach out to him.

I just wasn't sure that someone should be me.

"She said this happened outside of a coffee shop near his office." Lisa glanced back at the clock mounted over the door. "About twenty-five minutes ago. If you leave now you can probably catch him."

Maybe, but I couldn't force the guy to talk to me. "I can certainly head up there and ask to take his statement, but if he refuses..."

"Then I'll be able to enter that as part of the record."

In other words, get my butt up to Port Townsend and get some sort of response.

Fine. If Mr. Sweezy refused to talk, I'd have that much more time to cross the street and chat with a couple of appraisers I knew.

Chapter Twenty-One

"IS GRANT EXPECTING you?" asked the receptionist who had provided the cover story for him yesterday.

Since it was the only symbol of authority I had, I flashed my deputy coroner badge at her. "No, but it's important that I see him...today."

She blanched as if I'd whipped out a warrant for Grant Sweezy's arrest. "I...uh...hadn't realized that—"

"Why don't you let him know I'm here," I said, hoping she'd think that she didn't have any better option. As opposed to her telling me to come back with a subpoena.

With a nod, the receptionist pointed to a pair of cloth-covered chairs under a watercolor street scene of Port Townsend. "Have a seat and I'll let him know you're here."

I was buzzing with too much nervous energy to sit, so I stood in front of the watercolor like an unimpressed art critic while I racked my brain for a good reason this deputy coroner would want to question a commercial real estate broker.

Unfortunately, by the time the receptionist led me to a nearby conference room I hadn't come up with anything that Sweezy wouldn't immediately see through as the pathetic lie that it was.

"He'll be right with you," she said as if she hoped it were true, so I took that to mean that I should make myself comfortable.

Almost ten minutes of doodling on my notepad later, an attractive man in his forties, wearing a pressed white dress shirt and khakis, opened the door.

I noted gray flecks in thick finger-combed hair, a plain gold wedding band, and a cheap sports watch like Steve's that made me think he was a runner. Mr. Sweezy even had an earnest expression on his face, not at all resembling the Mr. Sleazy I had been expecting to step through that door.

I pushed out of my chair, and he closed in to give me a warm handshake. "Hello. Grant Sweezy."

"Charmaine Digby with the Chimacam County coroner's office," I said, figuring that I'd better not let on that I was the one he'd had the appointment with yesterday. At least not until I got some answers. "Thanks for making the time."

"Of course." He took the seat across the table from me. "What's this about?"

I had only one card I could play to keep him from calling my bluff. "It has come to the attention of our office that you knew Ted Skerrett, aka Theodore Skerrett."

Sweezy narrowed his blue-gray eyes. "I'm sorry, who?"

"Ted Skerrett. Mid-seventies. Fell to his death last week while hiking one of the county trails. Maybe you heard about it in the local news?"

"The story sounds familiar but not the name."

I didn't expect that Ted's name would ring any bells, but that was okay. I just needed to feed Sweezy enough information to satisfy his own curiosity about why I'd come to see him, and not raise any suspicion in the process. "He had recently come into some money, and it had been suggested that he reached out to you about an investment opportunity with a group you'd formed."

Since one of Sweezy's investment groups had been named in Lisa's suit, I gave myself a little high-five for maneuvering him into position to make that statement I'd come for.

Lowering his gaze, he shook his head. "I think you must have me mixed up with someone else, 'cause I haven't talked to anyone ..." Taking a deep breath, his expression brightened. "Oh, I know what the mixup is."

You do?

"It was his sister who came to see me," Sweezy said with an easy smile on his lips, as if he were taking pleasure in solving the convoluted puzzle I'd laid out in front of him. "Brenda, right?"

Holy cannoli!

"Yes, I believe that's her name." I jotted a note with a shaky hand. "When was it that she came to see you?"

"Last week. Thursday, I think."

Two days after receiving the estate evaluation from the Ivies. "And may I ask how much money she was talking about investing?"

"Half a mil. To start with anyway."

To start with? What the heck had they discovered in that house?

I stared across the table at him. "I didn't realize the family had that kind of money."

"She made it sound as if it were something new, and made it clear that she was just exploring some of the recommendations her financial planner had laid out."

For the first time since Grant Sweezy joined me at the table, that earnest look on his face had a little crack in it. Probably because he didn't want to admit that he couldn't get Brenda to sign on the dotted line.

"And that's the last time you saw her?" I asked.

"That's the one and only time." The easy smile had made a comeback. Sweezy clearly thought that we'd exhausted the subject of Brenda Proctor.

And he was right.

"Okay." I set down my pen so that I could give him my undivided attention. "Now let's talk about a conversation that you had with someone at a coffee shop this morning."

After Grant Sweezy dropped the mask of earnestness he'd been wearing and informed me of the dark place I could stick the statement I had asked him to provide, I jaywalked across the street to see what I could find out about the fortune Brenda had come into.

At the sound of the buzzer, Grace Ivie popped up like a prairie dog from behind her desk. "Oh, it's you."

I hadn't expected her to be happy to see me, so I approached with what I hoped would be enough goodwill for the both of us. "Good morning."

She squared her shoulders as if bracing herself for a fight. "If you're here to see my husband, you should have made an appointment because he's out doing an appraisal."

"Actually, I'm here to see you." The partner who appeared to be the keeper of their business records.

"I can't imagine why," Grace said after an awkward pause.

Then she wasn't trying because, based on what Grant Sweezy had told me, I could think of at least a half-million reasons.

I pointed at the chair by her desk. "Could we sit for a minute?"

Grace vented a little sigh of resignation. "Until a customer comes in."

Waiting for her to settle in her desk chair, I glanced at the striking image on her computer monitor. It looked a lot like a jade dragon similar to several I'd seen in the Asian Art Museum in San Francisco. "Research for an appraisal you're doing?"

She angled her monitor away from my line of sight. "We only discuss our appraisals with our clients."

"Has Brenda Proctor become a client since we last spoke?"

"No," Grace stated, her nostrils flaring as she punctuated her answer with a sniff of disdain.

"Then you have no client for the appraisal you did for Ted Skerrett."

"He was the client. The fact that he is now deceased doesn't change that."

It did for me. "That may be the case, but you must be aware by now that he died under some unusual circumstances, apparently leaving everything to his sister."

Grace's expression didn't change as she met my gaze, but her pupils dilated.

Yep, very aware.

"Plus, there is some question about the validity of his wife's will," I added, watching for a reaction. "Holly and Marc, her children, were effectively disinherited."

Breaking eye contact, Grace flattened her unpainted lips.

Based on that reaction, I wondered if she had already come to that conclusion.

"Mrs. Ivie, I understand that I'm asking a lot of you, but I'm just trying to do the right thing for all the parties involved. Is there any way that you can give me a copy of that appraisal?"

She shook her head. "Absolutely not. I'm shocked that you would even suggest such a thing."

It was worth a shot.

"Then let me ask you about the day you visited the house. Just to make sure I haven't missed anything for the report I need to turn in today."

Yes, I had just lied through my teeth. Again. And once again, for good reason.

Grace hugged her arms to her chest as if the prospect of answering my questions filled her with icy apprehension. "Fine."

Since I knew I wouldn't have much time, I decided to focus on what Grace might have seen or heard. "While you and Mr. Ivie were working in the house, were you aware of anyone else speaking with Mr. Skerrett or his sister?"

"No," she said sharply.

Okay, that matched what her husband had told me. "While you were there, did you see anything that caused you to think that Mr. Skerrett might be in danger?"

She blinked. "No."

No? That's not what the quirk at the corner of her mouth was telling me. "Are you sure?"

"Nothing happened at the house to cause me to think there might be trouble. Not until that younger woman approached our car."

"Holly, the stepdaughter there with her brother."

Grace nodded.

"She wanted you to know that some of the items you evaluated were hers."

I got another nod.

"Then what happened?" I asked.

"I'd seen this kind of situation more times than I can count."

"I'm sure it can get heated between family members."

Grace rolled her eyes. "*Heated* is probably the polite word for what I witnessed that day."

"I understand it got pretty ugly between Mr. Skerrett and Holly."

"That's when Lawrence started the car. We simply can't get involved in how the estate *should* be divided. Our jobs are to fairly determine the value of an estate. Beyond that ... well, that's when people should talk to their lawyer. Especially..."

Grace's mouth flat-lined again as she stared out the rain-splashed window.

Whatever she was remembering that day, it was something she didn't feel she could divulge.

And I really needed her to keep talking. "Especially?"

"Well ... when the estate includes something of great value—an unknown when the will was drawn up. That's something that can't be settled with a shouting match on a driveway."

"Yeah," I said, thinking about the advice Lisa had given me last Friday. "That's why I told Holly she needed a lawyer."

"So did I."

What? "When did you talk to her?"

Grace slanted me a sharp glance, looking at me as if I were the dimmest bulb in her store. "I'm not completely heartless. I couldn't just drive away without giving the girl some hope."

"Then, would you be willing to do one more thing for that family and give me a copy of the appraisal?"

After a second of hesitation, Grace turned to her computer monitor, and started making mouse-clicks. "The attorneys representing that family can make that request, not you."

Dang.

She rose to her feet, features pinched, her gaze darting back to her monitor as she brushed past me. "Now, if you'll excuse me. I have work to do."

With the way she was rushing toward the back room, I felt a sense of having been in this situation before. Only the last time someone had left me alone in a room as part of an obvious setup, I was newly divorced and being ambushed with a blind date.

Grace Ivie hadn't scurried away so that I could have time alone with a special someone, but rather a something. In fact, two somethings.

Two images, side by side, filled the LED widescreen. On the left, a London museum's webpage with a brief description of a gleaming gold on black seventeenth-century Japanese lacquer box. The other, while poorly lit so that its gold inlay didn't gleam quite as brightly, was clearly the museum piece's twin. And by its side on the hardwood floor, a glass case that looked very familiar.

Holy crap! The glass case held one of the geisha dolls I'd seen on display in that spare bedroom ... on this lacquer box.

I pulled out my cell phone and snapped several pictures of the images displayed on the monitor.

It wasn't until I zoomed in to capture the bit of text Grace had added under the picture that I actually read what she'd written.

Auction presale estimate: $3 million.

"Wow!" No wonder Lawrence Ivie wanted to sign Brenda as a client. The commission he'd earn at auction could be worth hundreds of thousands of dollars.

That explained how desperate he was to speak with Brenda at her brother's funeral.

It also explained why Brenda wasn't letting Marc or Holly into that house.

What it didn't explain was how Ted wound up at the bottom of that ravine.

Chapter Twenty-Two

AFTER I GOT back to the office, I typed up Grant Sweezy's short and not so sweet statement and emailed it to Lisa. With nothing else pressing, I spent the rest of the morning catching up on the filing while I tried to figure out what to do with the images I now had on my phone.

I had a feeling that every one of the attorneys working on the third floor would be quick to categorize those photos as evidence of motivation. In the event that we were discussing Ted Skerrett's murder case, which no one wanted to talk to me about, with the obvious exception of Lucille.

Since I couldn't run the risk of opening up that discussion at work, and I knew Steve wouldn't be eager to see me, much less hear about my informal investigation, I decided to seek counsel from the person I trusted most not to try to get me fired: my grandmother.

Standing in Gram's kitchen fifteen minutes later, I knew I had made the right decision. Because not only was she delighted to have the diversion of thinking about something besides a cancelled wedding, she offered to feed me lunch. Bonus!

While Gram opened a can of soup, I poured myself a cup of coffee. "Is Mom still asleep?"

"Haven't heard a peep out of her."

"Good." I didn't need her "peeping" down here while I tried to have a serious conversation with the matriarch of our family.

Gram arched an eyebrow. "Charmaine Digby, have a little compassion. Your mother has gone through quite an emotional ordeal."

Most of which was of her own making. "I know. I didn't mean it that way. It's just that I need this to be a private conversation."

"Sounds serious," Gram said, emptying the can into a saucepan.

"It is." Deadly serious.

"As in talk now and eat later serious?"

"Probably."

She turned the heat down under the soup, grabbed her coffee cup, and motioned for me to follow her to the kitchen table.

Lowering herself into her usual chair, Gram met my gaze as I sat next to her. "Please don't tell me that this has something to do with you and Stevie."

"It doesn't." And I hoped that it never would. "This is a work thing that I probably shouldn't know."

Okay, Steve would be quick to correct me that I definitely shouldn't have any knowledge of anything that could implicate someone in the murder of Ted Skerrett.

But he wasn't here.

"Are you saying this could get you into trouble?" Gram asked.

"No." Because that would make her worry that I'd

done something I shouldn't have, and then she'd call Steve, who would be sure to agree with her.

I took a quick slurp of coffee and then pushed it aside. "I'm not in trouble, but I could make some trouble for someone else if I say too much. So I'm not going to use any names, and I can't divulge any real specifics."

Gram leaned forward in her chair as if this were story time. "Okay."

"Let's say that Gramps intended for me to have some relic that had been in the family for two hundred years, but you remarried and your new husband decided that he wanted to give it to his sister."

"Do you know what the odds are of me remarrying at this age?"

"Probably only slightly less than what mine would be, but that doesn't matter for the purpose of—"

"You can't be serious," Gram said, placing her warm palm on my hand.

"I'm not my mother's daughter in that respect. Don't plan on rushing to the altar anytime soon. Now, back to this historical artifact—"

"Hold your horses. Does Steve know that you feel this way?"

This was so not the conversation I wanted to have. "Doesn't matter. Besides, he's in no rush to do anything, either." Especially after I told him that I didn't want to move in.

"Who's not in a rush?" Marietta asked, padding into the kitchen in a silk robe and bare feet. She squinted at me through swollen eyelids. "You haven't been speaking with Barry, have you?"

Gram pointed at the chair next to me. "For heaven's

sake, Mary Jo. Char was talking about Steve."

Not intentionally.

Yawning, my mother dropped into the chair. "What about him?"

"Nothing." Absolutely nothing I wanted to discuss with either one of them. "And we're getting completely off-subject."

"But it sounds like you two were talking about something important," Marietta said. "And I interrupted."

I set my coffee cup in front of her with the hope that it would keep her mouth occupied for the next few minutes. "No, we were done. In fact, I should get back to work."

"But you didn't finish telling me about ... you know." Gram lowered her voice. "That *private* matter."

My mother froze as she reached for the cup. "Okay, what's going on?"

It was definitely time to go. "Nothing."

"Come on," Marietta said between sips. "You're not the only one in this family perceptive enough to see when someone's lying."

Good grief.

I turned to Gram as I pushed out of my chair. "We'll talk later."

Marietta sucked in a breath. "Oh! This is about that private chat I had with Steve a few months ago, isn't it? He finally told you."

My mouth went dry with the knowledge that she was talking about the time she demanded to know his intentions. I hadn't wanted to know what he told her then, and I didn't want to know now.

"Mary Jo, stop talking," Gram commanded.

Marietta's puffy eyes narrowed as she met her mother's parental glare. "You said this was about Steve, not wanting to—"

"Mary Jo!" Gram slapped the table. "Not one more word."

I didn't need to be able to read my grandmother's body language to understand why she hadn't wanted Marietta to reveal what Steve had told her that night.

Because, for him, it was beyond feeling no sense of urgency to get married and start a family. He didn't envision himself sharing that future with me.

This came as no surprise. Not really. Because deep within the core of my heart, where soul-crushing truths could not be denied, I'd always known this.

But still, it wasn't any less crushing to have a mirror held to this truth in the harsh light of day.

My mother would be the first to admit that the light of day isn't kind to a tearful Digby, and unlike her I couldn't spend the rest of mine hiding out in this house while I waited for the swelling to go down. So I blinked away the hot tears searing the back of my eye sockets and glanced in the direction of the clock on the stove. "Oh, look at the time."

I grabbed my tote and headed for the door. "I need to go."

Marietta tsked. "Are you sure? It's barely noon."

I didn't care what time it was. I couldn't stay here, not if I wanted to have a prayer of holding it together.

"What about lunch?" Gram asked, calling after me.

I waved at her from the carport. "Can't stay. Got a meeting."

"I'm not sure I believe you, because you had time to

eat a few minutes ago."

True, but that was before I lost my appetite.

✳

I was climbing the white marble steps of the court-house when I saw Shondra staring down at me from the third-floor landing.

And she didn't look happy to see me.

"Something wrong?" I asked, my voice reverberating in the echo chamber of the stairwell.

Shondra's lips tightened with disapproval. "You tell me."

Uh-oh. "I don't know that I have anything to tell." Not that I wanted to admit to anyway. Not until I had some proof that Ted Skerrett's death was no accident.

She folded her arms, straining the seams of her houndstooth jacket. "No? 'Cause you look about as guilty as my nine-year-old when I catch him lyin' to me."

I had the sinking feeling that someone had called to complain about me. Given the obscenities Grant Sweezy had hurled at me before he stormed out of that confer-ence room, I guessed he had given our receptionist an earful.

Stepping onto the landing next to Shondra, I braced myself for impact. "I...uh...don't—"

"Never mind. If you don't want to tell me, I'm not gonna ask."

Whew.

"And by that relieved look on your face, it's clear I don't wanna know," Shondra said, leading the way to the heavy oak door on the right.

I hated that I was that transparent, but at least I wouldn't have to follow her to her office for an ass-chewing. I didn't want anyone to see me cry, least of all this warrior of a woman. Not because it signaled my emotional vulnerability, but it could be taken as an admission that my skin wasn't thick enough for this job.

And it probably wasn't, but I was for darn sure going to fake it until that day came.

I forced a smile. "It's personal stuff, so yeah. You don't want to know."

She shot me a sympathetic look as we passed the reception desk. "He'll figure out that he's supposed to apologize. Sooner or later the good ones always do."

Steve didn't have anything to apologize for. He'd been nothing but a good and trusted friend to me for most of my life, and the months together since he first kissed me had been the happiest that I had ever known.

It wasn't his fault that I now wanted more than he could offer.

Chapter Twenty-Three

I SPENT THE bulk of my afternoon doing busywork—filing, copying, cleaning. In other words, mindless grunt work.

I even managed to organize the supply closet to Patsy's exacting standards. Not that I was expecting an attagirl, but she did grunt her satisfaction when she popped in for a ream of paper (and to check up on me, of course).

It was a tiny positive, a crumb of goodwill, probably the most I could ever ask for from my harshest office critic.

Did I dare hope that her icy disdain of me could be thawing?

But then Patsy gave me a frigid look, making it crystal clear that it would take a lot more than some supply closet détente to thaw the Faraday ice cap. "Frankie wants to see you."

I was pretty sure I knew the reason why I was being summoned. Because the Grant Sweezy complaint had skipped Shondra and had gone straight to the top of the department food chain. "As in right now?"

Patsy's lips curled into a humorless smile. "As in

immediately."

Yep. Straight to the top after a brief layover at Patsy's desk.

With my pulse thundering in my ears, I followed Patsy down the hall and knocked on Frankie's open door.

"Come," Francine "Frankie" Rickard said without looking up from reading the file on her desk.

I didn't sense any tension in the room. No more than usual anyway, given the fact that she was scowling at a criminal case file. "You wanted to see me?"

Frankie glanced at me over her wireframe bifocals and pointed at one of the gold brocade high-back chairs opposite her desk. "Have a seat, Charmaine."

No smile. No polite chitchat.

Instead, I got a look of disappointment that felt like a punch to my gut.

"Did you go to Port Townsend this morning and pay a visit to ..." Frankie picked up a pink message slip from the short stack of paper by her phone. "Grant Sweezy of Mackey Investment Management?"

"Yes, to get his statement."

"He's claiming that you misrepresented yourself."

If I wanted to keep my job, I needed to choose my words very carefully. "I may have given him the impression that I was there in my capacity as a death investigator."

Frankie's blue-eyed gaze sharpened. "And why would you do that?"

"Because he stood me up yesterday, and his receptionist had proven that she was willing to lie for him, so I knew I had to approach them from a different angle or

I wasn't going to get the time of day."

"I see."

"It worked. I got a face-to-face with him."

"So it seems. Try to play it straight next time. We wouldn't want anyone to think that we had an open death investigation. Especially not any members of the Skerrett family." Frankie fixed me with a pointed stare. "Am I making myself clear?"

"Very clear."

She couldn't have made herself more clear. But it struck me that an opportunity had just opened up.

Especially now that the county coroner knew that I'd used Ted Skerrett as bait during my morning fishing expedition. "But would you like to know what information Mr. Sweezy offered up about Ted Skerrett's sister?"

A crease formed between Frankie's brows. "He knows the sister?"

I nodded. "Trying to sign her as a client—potentially a million-dollar account."

"Really." Frankie tapped an index finger, her *tell* that she was thinking. "Curious timing."

"That's what I thought."

"Quite a tidy sum of money, too."

"I know." I sat at the edge of my seat. "Ruth's kids told me that there wasn't much left at the time of their mother's death, so ..."

"There must have been an insurance policy they didn't know about."

"Or there was some treasure in the house that the sister discovered." With the help of the Ivies.

"Treasure's always a possibility." A smirk tugged at

the corner of Frankie's mouth. "Not terribly likely, though. Not too many pirates coming ashore in Gibson Lake to bury treasure."

I wanted to tell her it was more likely than she thought. Even if I was wrong, and the golden treasure chest in Ruth's spare bedroom had nothing to do with Ted falling to his death down that ravine, at least Frankie would be aware of everything that I'd learned in the past week.

She wouldn't be happy with me, and I'd surely get a sterner talking-to. But maybe, just maybe, I could provide her with enough circumstantial evidence to launch an official investigation into the death of Ted Skerrett.

And then her phone rang.

Frankie glanced at the caller ID and groaned. "I have to take this. Thank you, Charmaine."

Crap. I was being dismissed.

"Remember what we talked about," Frankie added as she picked up her phone.

I had a feeling what she'd remember: an assistant who wanted to believe in buried treasure and pirates.

I left her office determined to return with something more substantial than fantastical musings that made it sound like I'd been alone too long with a bottle of grog.

To do that, I needed the help of someone who had a lot to lose. She just had yet to realize how much was at stake.

Almost three hours later, I arrived at Holly Hines' north Seattle townhome at the same time as a pimply-faced pizza delivery guy.

The man in his early fifties who opened the door gave me a friendly nod after he handed a small wad of cash to the delivery dude. "You must be the reason my wife ordered pizza for dinner," he said.

And it smelled almost as good as Eddie's. "Probably. Is she home?"

"In the kitchen."

I followed him inside to a recently remodeled kitchen with gleaming dark granite, glass cabinets, and black high-end appliances, where the two teens I saw at Ted's funeral sat at the counter with some reality TV show blaring.

After giving me a cursory glance, they stared at the pizza box like hungry birds.

Not so with the mama bird in the canary yellow blouse setting the plates in front of them. Holly hadn't even acknowledged that I was in the room.

Not until she looked over while pouring herself a glass of wine. "Want one?"

I shook my head. "Got a long drive." And I needed to stay sharp.

"Okay. You've got this," Holly announced to her husband as she click-clacked past him in a pair of chunky heels.

"Want us to save you a slice?" he asked, already digging into the box.

"No." She shot me a look of disgust that I figured had more to do with eating greasy pizza than with talking to me.

But I was pretty sure Holly didn't want to do that either.

She extended a tapered finger toward the entryway and led me back to the sparsely furnished home office I had passed on my way in. "We can have some privacy in here."

"Okay." I didn't care about the location. I and the clenched gut I had developed on the ferry ride over here just needed to light the fuse on this conversation and get the ensuing explosion over with. Then I could determine if I'd found myself an ally.

While Holly closed the office double doors, I sat in the center of a cushy rose-patterned loveseat that coordinated perfectly with her red wine. "I take it by his absence that Marc won't be joining us," I said, hoping that would be the case because I didn't need her brother adding to the tension level in the room.

With a hard set to her mouth, she stalked to the mahogany desk. "You said you needed to speak to me in private." Holly eased herself into the desk chair, took a sip of wine, and leveled her gaze on me. "I assume this has to do with why I was told to get a lawyer."

I nodded. "It has everything to do with it."

She sucked in a ragged breath, dramatically releasing it. "There's something in that house, isn't there?"

And there was something in this room. Something in Holly's posture, her eager expression as she gripped a corner of the desk to brace herself that made the drama seemed forced, too over the top. Sort of like when Marietta had a recurring cameo role on a soap opera and then got skewered by the critics for overplaying her part.

Worse than the bad acting, Holly was asking the wrong question. Because she already knew there had to be something of value in the house. Grace Ivie as much

as said so when she advised Holly to hire an attorney—
the same day that Ted died.

"That's my understanding," I said, wondering if I
had made a horrible error in judgment by coming here.

Holly slammed her fist on the desk, almost knocking
over her wineglass. "Son of a ...! I knew that bastard was
up to something. Him and that evil sister of his."

The outrage was real, but I couldn't begin to believe
that Holly's blood had taken over a week to reach a
boiling point.

"Because the appraisers clued you in that day on the
driveway, right?" I asked, watching her carefully.

"One of them tried to, but good ol' Ted practically
chased them off the property before I could ask any
questions."

"Even if you hadn't arrived in time to see them drive
off, you would've thought something was up, wouldn't
you? I mean, Ted and Brenda weren't letting you inside
the house to clear out the stuff your mom had left you."

Holly furrowed her brows. "I suppose. But you never
suspect someone you've known for years of being that
devious."

Did she think I was stupid? "You must have, or you
and Marc wouldn't have rushed to Gibson Lake after
Ted called to let you know about the appraisal he'd
arranged."

She shrugged.

"Or chase after him when he took off to that trailhead." I leaned in to get a better view of her face. "Kinda
tells me you thought he was exactly that devious, and
that you weren't going to stand by and let him get away
with it."

Her eyes widened as if an internal alarm was sounding. "We just wanted to talk…to reason with him."

"And did you get that chance?"

"We already discussed this. Ted headed up that trail and Marc was in no condition to try to catch up with him."

True enough. "But you were."

Holly's jaw clenched as though she were trying to clamp down on the words threatening to escape from her mouth.

"As angry as you were at your stepfather trying to screw you out of your inheritance, you wouldn't let him just walk away from you." I had no idea how much she'd paid for the chunky heels she had on, but I was pretty sure they were a heck of a lot pricier than my discount rack clogs. And I didn't doubt for a second that she'd risk ruining them to get what was rightfully hers. "You left the car and went after him, didn't you?"

Holly's face reddened. "No! I told you—"

"Yeah, I know. You didn't want to ruin your three-hundred-dollar shoes."

"That's right. They were Jimmy Choos."

Nice try, but I happened to know how much Marietta paid for her Jimmy Choos, and three hundred bucks wouldn't even cover one foot. "We both know that's not true."

"But—"

"So tell me," I said, trying to sound more confident than I felt while my heart pounded as if I had just run up Spirit Rim. "What happened on that trail?"

Holly stared into the depths of her wineglass, her mouth a flat line.

"You might as well just say it, because I was able to track down the owner of one of those cars in the trailhead parking lot, and he saw you climbing up toward the rim."

That had been the biggest lie of the night, but I was counting on the fact that I was the only one in the room with an accurate BS meter.

With her elbows on the desk, Holly hung her head in her hands. "It's not the way it looks."

It looked pretty bad to me.

She was on the trail.

Ted was on the trail.

Then, he fell to his death from the trail.

Not only pretty bad, seriously bad.

"Would you like to tell me what happened, or should I ask Detective Pearson to call on you?" As if I could get him to reopen his inquiry without first running it past Frankie.

Holly's shoulders slumped. "Nothing happened."

"Something must have happened. Ted ended up dead."

"Not because of anything I did," she insisted, her voice breaking. "I never even saw him after he took off running."

I didn't get the sense she was lying, but I needed her to sit up and repeat that to my face to be sure.

I pushed away from the loveseat and stood next to her. "Are you telling me that you couldn't keep up with him?"

Holly extended her leg so that I could see the three-inch heels she was wearing. "Not a great substitute for running shoes."

Not only true but reasonable. "Did Ted say anything before he took off?

"Other than 'Go home' and a few choice expletives, no."

"Then what?"

"Then nothing," Holly said, her volume rising. "He disappeared around a bend, and I walked back to the car."

What goes up should come down. So assuming that she didn't know that Ted had taken a tumble, she should have waited in that parking lot for him.

I smiled sympathetically. "Probably in some rainy muck, right?"

"Yeah, I had to watch my step. It was a little slippery."

"So you're wet, maybe a little muddy. I imagine you wanted to beat it to the six-thirty ferry and get home to clean up."

"I wasn't going anywhere. Not until I made Ted understand that we weren't going to stand idly by and let him take advantage of us." Holly vented a wine-scented breath that sounded like a low growl. "But my brother informed me that he had to go to the bathroom, so I never got the chance to ... Not that it would have made any difference if we'd stayed."

Sadly, it seemed that she was speaking the truth. Except if she and Marc had staked out the parking lot a little longer, they might have seen someone else come down from the trail.

Since Holly couldn't tell me anything else about what she'd seen that night, I only had one last question to ask her. "Did you get a lawyer?"

"My brother and I talked to one this morning. Marc has another lawyer buddy that he thought might give us a family and friends discount. We're seeing him tomorrow."

"Good. Just make a decision soon, and tell him to call Grace Ivie to get a copy of the appraisal."

Holly's gaze sharpened. "Have you seen it?"

"No." And I didn't trust her enough to share the photo of what I had seen. "But get a good lawyer as soon as you can."

'Cause you're gonna need one.

Chapter Twenty-Four

"YOU DON'T WANT to do this," Rox said, scowling at me from behind the bar instead of delivering my pizza order to the kitchen. "Not after you've been so good all these weeks."

I didn't want or need my best friend to turn into my diet coach. I already had a carb-conscious, calorie-crusading mother eager to bestow her body image wisdom, and no doubt imbue me with an eye-twitch in the process.

Besides, I hadn't had anything to eat since my breakfast with Steve. Aside, of course, from the two candy bars I ate an hour ago on the ferry. And if I wanted to look for some edible relief from this dreadful day in a cheese pizza, I was in no mood to have the happiest person I knew get in my face about it.

I leaned in to be heard over the Mariners fans yelling at the flat screen mounted on the wall behind me. "Do I need to take the order in there myself?"

Rox parked her hands at her hips. "Not if you tell me why now, after all this time, you're falling off the wagon."

I hung my head. "Trust me, my dieting wagon has

had some wobbly wheels for a while now."

"But the dress you need to fit into for your mom's wedding—"

"There's not going to be a wedding."

"What? Why?"

I looked around. Several empty seats separated me from the three guys in matching bowling league shirts sitting near the taps at the center of the bar, so with Aerosmith blaring through the overhead speakers, I didn't have to worry about being overheard. "This has to remain just between you and me, so no telling Donna. Okay?"

Rox solemnly nodded.

"Marietta called it off."

"Whoa. I thought you were going to tell me that Barry Ferris came to his senses and realized he was making a huge mistake."

I shook my head. "Nope, not yet. But I think that's one of the many things my mother is afraid of right now."

"Well, I guess I don't need to worry about looking like a stuffed sausage in that preggers dress we found a couple weekends back in Port Townsend."

"Speaking of sausage," I said, pointing toward the kitchen door. "Why don't you add some of that to my pizza order."

She aimed another scowl at me. "You eating in or is this to go?"

"I have a hungry dog at home. Better not keep him waiting."

"Keep who waiting?" Steve asked, sliding onto the barstool next to me.

Criminy. Steve was the last person I wanted to talk to tonight. "My furry date."

"Hunh." He smiled at Rox as she tossed a coaster in front of him. "I thought I might be your date."

"I'm spoken for," she quipped. "Want a beer as a consolation prize?"

"Sure." Dropping the smile the second Rox stepped toward the taps, Steve leaned close. "Where have you been? I've been trying to reach you."

"Oh, yeah?" He couldn't have been trying very hard, because my phone hadn't once rung or buzzed with a message since my mother called while I was driving through Seattle traffic to Holly's house. "Well, it so happens that I was working."

And needed to concentrate.

And Marietta kept calling, so I turned off my phone.

Shoot. I reached into my tote to press the *on* button.

"I even left you a couple messages," he said, observing me a little too carefully. "And since you appear to be turning on your phone, I'm going to assume you didn't hear that I was hoping we could have dinner tonight."

"I've made other plans."

"And I grabbed a sandwich when I didn't hear back from you."

"Then what are you doing here?" I asked while Rox set a tall, foamy glass in front of him. "Out of beer at home?"

Clearly unamused, Steve leveled his gaze on me. "I was coming back from a call and saw your car parked out front."

On the nights I wanted to let my fat cells find some solace in a gooey pizza, I needed to remember to park in the back.

"You ordering anything from the kitchen?" Rox asked Steve.

He turned to me. "What're you having?"

None of this ridiculously awkward conversation. That's what I was having.

Grabbing my tote, I got to my feet. "Actually, I just stopped in for a minute because I needed to have Rox talk me out of something."

She cocked her head and looked at me the way Fozzie does when I tell him all about my day. Confused, impatiently waiting for me to say something about food. "Does that mean that you don't want the—"

"Nope." Not while I had an audience to pass judgment on my need for cheese, I didn't. I just wanted to go home.

I reached across the bar to give her a hug. "Thanks. See you soon."

Steve downed half the glass and threw some cash on the bar. "I'll go with you."

"Stay and finish your beer." I tried to steer him back to his seat when he stepped in front of me. "I'll see you tomorrow."

He took me by the elbow and led me toward the door. "You'll see me now."

"Steve, be nice," Rox called after us. "She's not in a good mood."

I glared up at him. "Yeah, what she said."

Steve picked up the pace. "Then that makes two of us."

"So let me go and let's talk tomorrow," I said over the thunderous cacophony of balls and scattering pins as I pushed through the front door.

"I'll be happy to talk to you tomorrow as soon as you tell me what your problem is."

Standing under the entry canopy while a misty breeze cooled my overheated cheeks, I yanked my arm away from him. "*My* problem! You're the one at breakfast who acted like he couldn't get away from me fast enough."

His eyes were hard as stone. "I had to get to work."

"Yeah. That's what you said."

"So that's what you're mad about?"

"I'm not mad."

"Then how about pissy?"

I stalked toward my car so that I wouldn't say something I'd regret. "Now you're just being a jerk."

"Really," he said, following me. "You're just going to walk away."

"I'm walking away because there isn't anything left to say, except..." I turned, gusts of wind whipping tendrils of hair in front of my eyes as I reached out to him.

Steve's gaze softened at my touch. "Char—"

With my palms caressing the rough planes of his face, I silenced him with a gentle kiss while he wrapped his arms around me.

While I hesitated to say anything to spoil the moment, my heart had been aching for too many hours to not address the wedge threatening to split it apart.

I rested my cheek against his neck. "I'm sorry if I hurt you this morning. It's just important to me to be able to live on my own right now."

"What do I have to say to convince you that I understand that?" he asked with a level of exasperation that seemed really uncalled for, considering that I was the one doing the apologizing.

I pushed against his solid chest. "Then why did I get the silent treatment?"

He gave me a cop squint. "Remember me going outside to take a call?"

I nodded.

"I was being informed that a witness in one of my cases had shown up at the station looking for me."

"At seven in the morning?"

"I don't get to pick the timing of when things happen. I was just wondering why he picked this morning to come in."

I swatted his arm. "That's what you were brooding about?"

"Hey, I wasn't brooding. I was thinking about what would be waiting for me when I got in."

"Well, next time why don't you give me more of a clue what you're thinking about so that one of us doesn't get accused of getting pissy about it!"

"You want a clue?" Steve pulled me close and pressed his lips against mine.

Leaning into him, I linked my hands behind his neck and savored the taste of him, the delicious feel of his body against mine.

I soaked in his warmth, my inner core melting like butter. Then, just as I thought I might dissolve into the wet gravel by our feet, Steve broke off the kiss.

"Did I give you enough of a clue what I'm thinking about?" he asked, his breath warm on my ear.

"Mmmm, maybe. Why don't you give me another clue just to make sure."

✳

In the five minutes that it took to drive to my apartment, my mother called. That came as no surprise, since she'd already left me three voice messages that I hadn't worked up the energy to deal with on an empty stomach. But seconds after I didn't answer, she issued a parental edict in the form of a text.

GET HOME IMMEDIATELY.

I knew Marietta would hound me all night like a dog on a scent if I didn't shut off my phone. For most of my adult life, that had been my temporary solution of choice to keep from getting dragged into the latest crap sandwich of my mother's making.

But now that eleven hundred miles no longer separated us, I was pretty sure that it would be just a matter of minutes before she came over to deliver that sandwich in person. So I told Steve that I'd meet him in an hour at his house.

I figured that would give me enough time to feed Fozzie, wolf down some leftovers, and then take him for a walk before heading over to Gram's. And after doing some quick primping in front of my bathroom mirror, I arrived at my grandmother's back doorstep with seven minutes to spare.

Perfect.

Because I didn't want to devote any more time than that to the latest melodrama to unfold in Marietta's life saga. Not when I had some make-up sex waiting for me across the street.

"Hello," I called out after using my key to let myself in.

The kitchen was dark, but I could hear voices in the living room, where a glow of dim light flickered. So when I heard no answer, I expected to find Gram asleep like usual in front of her television set.

Yep, sound asleep and snoring with my mother nowhere to be seen, so I made my way upstairs to get this installment of the Marietta Moreau show over with.

"Mom?" I said from the top step.

"Chahmaine?" She came to the doorway of my old bedroom and planted her hands at her tiny waist. "Well, it's about time you showed up. Where have you been?"

I wasn't in the mood to indulge any of her latent maternal tendencies, and that included accounting for my whereabouts. "Working. You rang?"

She vented a breath of annoyance as I angled past her. "Several times."

"What's up?" I asked, noticing that three of the new outfits she had acquired on her recent trip to Los Angeles were spread out on the quilted comforter. "Are you going somewhere?"

Marietta beamed as if she had swallowed a ray of sunshine. "I'm going on a honeymoon!"

You can't be serious. "The wedding's back on?"

She threw her arms around me. "I wanted you to be the first to know. You're not, of course, because I couldn't reach you, so I rushed back to share the good news with your grandmother. But you're the second."

I didn't care about coming in second. I was only interested in what had transpired in the last nine hours to transform the miserable, unemployed actress consumed with the fear of adding to her long list of bad decisions back into a blissfully ecstatic bride-to-be.

I stepped out of her embrace so that I could see her face. "Rushed back from where?"

Marietta's extended lashes brushed her cheeks as her glossy lips parted in a coy smile. "Barry's. I went over to talk to him."

I knew Gram wouldn't have let Marietta drive her SUV, not after crashing two cars and Duke crowning her with the family nickname of "Mayhem" Moreau.

So if she rushed back to tell Gram her news, my grandmother obviously didn't give Marietta a ride over to Mr. Ferris's house, and I certainly didn't. Although it was a safe bet that's what her first call to me was all about.

Since I'd never known her to go outside the family to bum a ride... "Don't tell me you walked over there."

Marietta shot me a mischievous look. "No, silly. When you didn't answer your phone, I called Steve and he gave me a ride."

Stifling a groan, I dropped to the bed. "You didn't." Because I was never going to hear the end of this.

"He was very nice about it," she said, moving a plum silk blouse to sit next to me. "Said he had to go out that direction anyway. But really, I think it was because he knew we needed to talk."

What?

I couldn't have heard that right. "You mean you and Barry needed to talk."

"Well, obviously that too."

Propping my knee on the bed, I turned to face her. "Why would Steve need to talk to you?" And not mention a thing about it to me.

"Because he cares about you, and I am your mother, so it's only natural that he would turn to me."

I stared at her in disbelief. "Like for advice?"

"Of course."

This wasn't natural. Since I knew that Steve only tolerated Marietta because she was my mother, this was some alternative-universe crazy talk coming out of her mouth.

Even more crazy, I didn't get the sense she was lying.

"And what on earth did you tell him?" I asked, my voice mainly breath.

Marietta patted my cheek. "Don't you worry about what I told him."

Oh, sure. Today of all days, I wasn't to worry about another private conversation between my marriage-minded mother and my sex buddy/boyfriend.

"Just trust me, everything about my idea to talk it out with Barry was all good." She grinned. "In every not-so-little respect, if you know what I mean."

Having a heart-to-heart talk with him had been my idea, but I didn't care to debate that point with her or listen to Marietta expound about any of Mr. Ferris's particulars.

I just wanted to know one thing. "So you cleared the air. You talked about moving into that big house he wasn't crazy about you buying, and you living a quieter lifestyle up here."

Marietta averted her gaze, smoothing out a wrinkle that didn't exist in the blouse behind her. "We talked."

I took that as a *no*. "Mom."

"I said we talked, and I mean it."

"Okay. I just know that when I left last night, you were convinced that it would be a big mistake to—"

"We worked all that out, so don't give a second thought to anything I said." Easing off the bed, she waved her hand as if it held a magic wand to make the memory of last night go away. "That was just the wine and some pre-wedding jitters talking."

Uh-huh. "You're absolutely certain of that."

"Absolutely, positively."

"Because if you want to live in that house for a while and make very sure that you can see a future here with Barry, I'm sure he'd understand if you postponed the wedding for a few months."

Marietta snatched up the blouse, gripping it as if it were a lifeline. "Chahmaine, I've already kept him waiting months, and neither one of us wants to wait a minute longer."

"I guess it's settled, then."

"It's completely settled. And the wedding will be Saturday, just like we planned."

Then there wasn't anything else to talk about, not when I had a hot date that might start cooling off if I didn't hurry up and get my hiney across the street.

"Good," I said, shooting Marietta my brightest fake smile as I pushed off the bed. "I'm happy for you."

She blinked away the tears threatening to make a sudden reappearance and reached for my hand. "Thank you. That means a lot."

Yeah, she could tell when I was lying, all right.

I tried to pull my hand back. "Well, I should go."

"Not just yet," she said, tightening her grasp. "We still have a certain house to discuss."

Chapter Twenty-Five

AFTER KISSING STEVE good night around eleven, I drove back to my apartment and wrote out a list of pros and cons of moving into Mr. Ferris's house.

By the time I hit the sack, I had seven good reasons to move there in the *pro* column and one line item that trumped them all on the *con* side of the page: my mother as my landlord. But when I woke up a couple hours later to the sound of my noisy next-door neighbors arguing about some missing rent money, I knew I had omitted a critically important *pro*: We would no longer share a bedroom wall.

"What do you think we should do, Fozzie?" I asked the dog sharing my bed.

He responded by leaping to the floor and heading out the door as if casting a vote to get the heck out of Dodge.

I kicked off the covers and followed him into the kitchen. "Yours is not the deciding vote, you know."

I didn't necessarily disagree with him, especially when I heard something that sounded like a shoe hitting the wall. So, once I'd downed a couple cups of coffee and tucked my hair under a ball cap, we set out into the predawn drizzle to take one more look at my mother's dream house. The one that had great potential to become a nightmare for me.

With Fozzie leading the way up the hill on 2nd Street, it struck me how quiet it was uptown as opposed to downtown near the truck route. Other than the birds chirping to greet the dawn and a handful of residents hitting the road to start their day, I didn't hear much of anything until the dog patrolling the fenced yard on our left started barking.

Then, standing across the street from where we had parked last Thursday, Fozzie shook off the droplets coating his fur and looked back at me as if he had been rained on long enough and wanted to go home.

"I know," I told him. "I feel the same way."

Because my decision had just been made.

After checking my work messages almost three hours later, I pulled out my cell phone and texted Mr. Ferris to ask if we could meet privately sometime after five.

No sooner than I hit *send*, my phone started ringing.

At first I thought that it couldn't be a good sign that Mr. Ferris felt the need to call me so quickly.

Only it wasn't him. It was Lucille calling from the Duke's kitchen phone.

"I've figured it out," she announced loudly enough for me and everyone else in the cafe to hear.

Fortunately I currently had the file wing of the third floor to myself. "Figured what out?"

"Who bumped off Ted, of course."

I could hear Duke in the background and knew that

he'd be adding a few choice words to the volume of this call if I didn't cut it short. "Why don't I come for lunch and you can tell me all about it."

"It has to do with our rich widows theory," she sang out as an enticement.

I sat up ramrod straight in my desk chair. "You've got a new angle on that?"

"You'd better believe it, and it's a doozy."

"I'll be right there," I said, grabbing my tote.

"Aren't you supposed to be at work?" Alice asked when I stepped through Duke's back door.

I flashed her a smile as I walked past her work table. "I'm on a coffee break."

"But it's barely eight o'clock!"

"I thought I'd take my morning break first and get it over with. My day is so much more productive that way."

Duke glowered over his shoulder at me. "No one's day is more productive with you rushing over here to join in the gabfest."

I patted the old sourpuss's back. "I won't be long. I promise."

Mainly because I knew that if I didn't come right back with the office supplies I told Patsy that we needed, I would no longer have a job to deliver them to.

Scanning the dining room for Lucille while I made my way to the coffee station, I spotted her, order pad in hand, at the booth Steve and I sat in yesterday.

"Shouldn't you be somewhere else right about now?" Stanley asked, pushing his empty cup toward me.

"I'm out getting some stuff for the office," I told him

while pouring his decaf.

He folded the newspaper in front of him. "Duke carries office supplies now?"

"No. I just needed to stop by and pick something up first."

Chuckling, Stanley reached for the sugar. "Catch up on the latest gossip from the gaggle in the corner is more like it."

"And you've got three minutes to do it. Tops." Duke aimed his spatula at the waitress squeaking toward the pass-through window with a gleam in her eye. "'Cause I'm not paying anyone to sit around and flap their gums."

"Some customers come in because they know I'll make time to chat with them as opposed to certain grumps in this establishment," Lucille retorted, tacking an order ticket on the wheel in front of Duke. "So you should actually be thanking me for putting butts in those seats."

The grump's expression darkened. "Yeah, right. Remind me to send you a thank-you note." Duke shot me a glance. "Three minutes."

"Yes, sir." But he and I both knew that holding the Queen of Gossip Central to a lightning round-type conversation was going to be tough.

I closed the distance between us so that I could whisper in Lucille's ear. "Talk fast. What did you find out?"

Grabbing a couple of mugs and a steaming carafe of coffee, she motioned for me to follow her. "You'll want to hear this from the horse's mouth."

Since we were heading toward the corner table,

where three familiar faces were looking at me as if I had been keeping them waiting, I figured the horse in this case was wearing a heather gray sweatshirt.

"Okay, now that she's finally here," Lucille said, pointing at me to sit in the empty chair next to Carmen. "I'm gonna do a quick recap to bring her up to speed."

As a reminder I held up three fingers. "Make it really quick."

"Fine." She splashed some coffee into all the empty cups at the table. "We know that Ted asked Winnie to marry him just weeks after Ruth passed. What if she wasn't the only one he popped the question to?"

Carmen turned to me. "And before you ask, it wasn't me."

Based on what she'd told me last week, I knew that wasn't because of a lack of trying on her part.

"No offense, Carmen," Lucille said, dropping into the chair to my right. "It seems that good ol' Ted was only in the market for ladies with plenty of money."

Ignoring Carmen's heavy sigh, Lucille looked across the table at Nadine. "Tell her about Delia."

That was a name I hadn't heard before today. "Who?"

Nadine pursed her lips as she stirred a creamer into her coffee. "Delia Edgerton, Ted's first wife. From all accounts, she was a well-heeled cougar who was as much of a flirt as he was."

Sylvia, a friend of my grandmother's, sitting next to Lucille, leaned in as if she hadn't heard correctly. "A what?"

"An older woman who seeks out the company of younger men," I offered to keep the conversation moving forward.

"You mean for S-E-X?" Sylvia whispered.

Lucille rolled her eyes. "What do you think?"

Sylvia patted her silver bouffant hair. "Maybe I should look into that."

Carmen hooted. "Honey, let me know when you want to go clubbing and I'll go with you."

We were careening down a path I didn't want to travel, so I thought I'd better pull us back with the obvious question that needed to be answered. "Was Delia a widow?"

"A fairly recent one when she married Ted." Nadine glanced at the redhead next to her. "At least that's what I remember Ruth telling us."

Carmen nodded. "And Delia had a bit of money because her first husband was a pediatrician—"

"Periodontist," Nadine corrected.

Carmen's lips thinned. "Whatever. All I know is that she had a bundle. Nice house in Port Townsend, too. Pretty sure that's why Ted retired as early as he did. 'Cause he must've thought he had it made."

"Okay." I failed to see how this trip down memory lane accomplished anything beyond solidifying Lucille's rich widow theory. "So Ted might have been a bit of a gigolo in his younger days."

Sylvia scoffed. "A bit. It sounds like he wanted to be a kept man."

"That's absolutely what he wanted," Lucille said between loud slurps of coffee. "But he messed with the wrong woman."

I locked gazes with her. "What's that supposed to mean?"

Lucille shrugged. "It's obvious. At least once you factor in that proposal to Winnie."

Not to me it wasn't. "You're not suggesting that Winnie—"

"Don't be ridiculous." Lucille's coral-painted lips quirked into a little sneer as she looked across the table at Carmen. "But Ted wasn't exactly a paragon of virtue while he was courting our pal Winnie."

"Excuse me, but I wasn't informed that they were going steady," Carmen protested.

"That's because you don't broadcast what you're doing when you're hedging your bets." Lucille turned to me. "Especially if you're getting desperate for money, which seems pretty dang safe to assume from the way he was pressuring Winnie to tie the knot."

"So you think there was another woman in the picture." I typically wasn't quick to jump to any of the same conclusions as Lucille. But this one not only seemed reasonable, it helped explain why Ted didn't try to change Winnie's mind after she told him she couldn't see him anymore. "Another source of funds in case Winnie didn't say yes."

Lucille folded her arms under her ample breasts and nodded with satisfaction. "Find her and you'll find the person responsible for Ted taking a tumble off that trail."

Right. Easy-peasy.

"How would you begin to look for this person?" Sylvia asked. "Assuming she even exists."

I had no idea. Because in a retirement mecca like Port Merritt, that would be like looking for a needle in a haystack. Maybe a gold-plated needle, but still...

"Oh, she exists, all right," Lucille said. "And just like we found out about Winnie, we'll find out about her."

Only if this mystery woman happened to wander in here during Lucille's shift and get all misty-eyed about Ted.

The odds of that kind of dumb luck seemed as likely as one of Lucille's conspiracy theories panning out, so I pushed away from the table to exit the gabfest. "Thanks for your time, ladies. Please let me know if you hear any rumors about Ted seeing other women. But let's not mention this to anyone else." Especially anyone I worked with.

Four heads nodded.

"So? Whaddya think?" Lucille asked, following me into the kitchen. "Pretty good possibility we're gonna crack the case, huh?"

Duke grunted as we passed by the grill. "The only good thing about that conversation was that you kept it under five minutes."

"Never mind him," I told Lucille. "I appreciate the information." Mainly because it gave me a lead I wanted to follow up on with the woman who knew Ted the best—his twin.

Chapter Twenty-Six

I RACED BACK to the office after picking up a can of coffee and filters, and only had to suffer a withering look from Patsy when I told her that I decided to grab a sandwich while I was at the store.

As if a brief stopover at the Red Apple deli counter could make up for the side trip I'd taken to see Lucille.

"No one asked about your lunch plans, Charmaine," Patsy flatly stated without sparing me a second glance.

Fine by me.

Even better, no one assigned me anything other than an hour-long copying project. So the second that the courthouse clock struck noon, I was free to jump in my car and make good on a message that I'd left on Brenda's answering machine.

I'd been careful to mention only that there had been a development in her brother's case. I figured that would provide enough enticement to buy a few minutes of Brenda's time.

When I pulled into the driveway of the Gibson Lake home and saw her give me a little wave from the front porch, I relaxed in the knowledge I had been right.

"I wasn't expecting to hear from you again," Brenda

called out to me as I approached.

I aimed my best poker face at her. "Some new information has come to light that I wanted to discuss with you."

Brenda froze as if she were hearing alarm bells.

I had a feeling that she must have received a recent call from Holly and Marc's new attorney, and I tucked away the startled look on Brenda's face as a card I could use later.

"Come on then," she muttered. "Let's see what you got."

I followed Brenda to the living room, expecting that I would once again be surrounded by dolls staring down at us with lifeless eyes. But the shelf mounted above the sofa was now empty.

"Did Mrs. Skerrett's children stop by to pick up some of their things?" I asked, taking a seat on the center cushion.

Brenda's lips thinned into a razor-fine line. "Not yet."

Since her body language was shouting "over my dead body," I had no doubt that she had heard from that attorney.

She eased herself into the wingback chair across from me. "About this new information—does it have something to do with those two opportunists?"

That sounded a lot like the pot calling the kettle black. Since I didn't dare let on that I knew anything about the art treasure down the hall, I tried to shift my facial expression into neutral. "I'm not sure I know what you mean."

Brenda shook her head. "Never mind. Just tell me

the news."

I scooted my butt to the edge of the sofa cushion to get a better read of Brenda's face. "It's come to our attention that your brother had intended to walk the trail with Winnie Dearborn the night he died."

Brenda's gaze intensified. "So?"

I saw plenty of annoyance, but not so much as a crumb of surprise. "So if his date cancelled on him, from people I've talked to it seems that Ted could have been with another lady friend that night."

Crossing her arms, she shrugged. "He and Ruth had a lot of friends. Good friends, bringing over cakes and casseroles long after Ruth's funeral. Even though I was perfectly capable of feeding my own brother."

Winnie and the other ladies had probably assumed that Brenda would have gone back home after her position as Ruth's caregiver was no longer needed, leaving her twin to fend for himself. "I'm sure their hearts were in the right place."

Or in Carmen's case, she was probably wearing hers on her sleeve.

"I suppose." A corner of Brenda's mouth quirked with contempt. "But some of those girls don't always take the hint that you don't need another flippin' tuna casserole."

I knew that was a reference to the can of tuna Sylvia would buy every time there was a local funeral reception. As a pensioner she didn't fit the wealthy widow profile, so I couldn't imagine Ted showering her with much attention.

"Who didn't take the hint?" I asked, hoping that Brenda would name names.

"Pretty much all of 'em."

"Did you get the impression that any of the ladies wanted to spend more time with Ted? You know, beyond sharing a piece of cake."

She glanced down at her tan bootie slippers "Nope."

Her answer was a little too cavalier, too dismissive, considering the fact that we were discussing who could have been with Ted the evening that he died.

"So no one that he mentioned seeing when he was out and about?"

Brenda scowled like she wanted to stick one of those booties up my butt. "Teddy had just lost his wife. Trust me, he wasn't out looking for another one."

I didn't trust Brenda as far as I could throw her, and not because I knew she had just lied to me—again. But I nodded to play along and kept my mouth shut about his proposal to Winnie. "Sometimes it's not about getting remarried, though. It's the companionship. Speaking for myself, it can be an adjustment being single again."

"Teddy never lacked for companionship."

Okay. That seemed true enough.

I waited for her to elaborate. When she didn't, I offered up the obvious clarification. "Female companionship."

"Like I said, he had friends."

"Any *friends* that he might have invited to join him on the trail that night?"

"I doubt it."

"Why?"

"He wasn't leaving because he had a hot date. He'd just had enough of Holly and Marc ..." Brenda's brow furrowed while her mouth clamped shut.

Yep, you were wandering into a danger zone. "I'm sorry," I said, acting as if I hadn't noticed. "I don't understand. Are you referring to the argument they got into with Ted?"

"Absolutely. Those two were making such a horrible scene that I thought we might have to call the police."

"So you're saying that Ted picked that time to hit the trail because he didn't want the situation to escalate."

"Exactly."

Sure. "Was this before or after Holly and Marc realized that they needed a lawyer?"

Brenda's face flushed as if she were ready to spew fire. "My brother was the one who got killed. Not them, so I resent you makin' them sound like they're so innocent, especially when they went driving after Teddy like they wanted to mow him down."

"If you were so concerned about him, why didn't you go after them to make sure he didn't get hurt?"

"I called and warned him they were coming. Beyond that, I thought he could take care of himself."

"You actually spoke to Ted?" Because I thought that the trail area was in a dead zone.

"Just for a few seconds before he lost signal."

"Did he mention if he saw anyone?"

"The only thing he said was to not worry." Brenda's dark eyes gleamed like a frozen lake. "I had a bad feeling he wasn't taking those two seriously enough, and now..."

And now, she didn't have her twin brother to worry about anymore.

I felt sorry for her loss. But given everything that she and her brother had been doing to cheat *those two* out of their inheritance, I wasn't *that* sorry.

✳

Checking my messages as I got into my car, I was pleased to see that Mr. Ferris was available to meet at five-thirty. But when that time finally rolled around, it was Marietta who greeted me at his front door.

"Well, hello there," she said, her green eyes glinting with delight.

"I didn't know you'd be here." I glanced behind her at the biology teacher giving me a sheepish look. *Since I had asked you for a private meeting.*

Closing the door, my mother linked her arm in mine. "A little bird told me that you might be stopping by."

"He also tried to drive you home an hour ago," Mr. Ferris said as Marietta led me into the adjoining living room.

She flicked her wrist as if she were shooing away a gnat. "We don't want to start our life together keeping secrets from one another. Now, do we, my darling?"

Instead of responding to her loaded question, he aimed an apologetic smile at me. "Sorry, Charmaine."

"Don't be silly. There's nothing to be sorry for." My mother took a seat on the oatmeal tweed sofa centered in front of a large picture window and patted the cushion next to her. "So what brings you over here? As if I couldn't guess."

She had just made the question I had wanted to ask Mr. Ferris a thousand times more complicated. "I wanted to talk to Barry about the rental," I said, planting my butt in the leather recliner in the corner so that I wouldn't be within striking distance of my volatile mother.

She rested her palm on Mr. Ferris's knee as he settled next to her on the sofa. "Wonderful. But let's not refer to this as a rental, Chahmaine. Because we wouldn't be charging you rent."

"We can talk about that. But first..." I locked gazes with Mr. Ferris. "Are you sure that you want me and Fozzie to live in your home?"

He folded his arms like a defiant teenager. "It's fine."

It didn't look so fine.

I pointed at his newly refinished entryway. "That hardwood is bound to get scratched."

"It's fine," he repeated with a little more volume.

The trouble with someone saying something louder is that it doesn't make it any more true. "You know I don't believe you, right?"

"Chahmaine, if Barry said it's fine, then it's perfectly fine."

And that was exactly why I hadn't wanted her here. "You don't have to do me any favors," I told him. "No matter what my mother says."

Marietta slammed her stiletto-clad foot to the carpeted floor, creating little more than a dull thud, but there was no mistaking that she had just issued a warning. "What exactly is that supposed to mean?"

Mr. Ferris blew out a breath. "Let's not raise our voices."

"Then let's have a reasonable conversation so that I don't have to," she said, narrowing her eyes at me.

That wasn't going to be possible as long as she kept opening her mouth. "Mom, I love you, but you need to stay out of this."

"Why should I?" She shot a green-eyed glare at her

future husband as if daring him to pick a side. "This is a family matter."

"And everyone needs the opportunity to speak openly." Not the least of which, the owner of the house.

"This is ridiculous," Marietta blustered. "Who's stopping anyone from speaking their mind?"

Mr. Ferris and I both stared at her.

Her jaw dropped. "I most certainly am not!"

He got to his feet and offered her his hand.

She recoiled as if he'd dangled a disembodied limb in front of her nose. "What are you doing?"

"I'd like you to watch TV in the bedroom for a few minutes," he stated in the same unyielding tone he used years ago, when he confiscated the girly magazine Eddie had smuggled into class.

She blinked, her expression softening. "But I wanted to be here to help—"

"I know." He pulled her up. "But I think you can help the most by giving Char and me some time alone."

"Fine," she said, slowly shuffling out of the room like a child being sent to her room without supper. But before she left, my mother turned to me. "You and I will talk about this later."

Not if I can help it.

Draping his arm around Marietta's shoulder, Mr. Ferris guided her toward the hallway. Then, seconds after I heard a door slam, he returned to the living room. "You want a beer, Charmaine?"

I didn't know if it would make the conversation we needed to have any easier, but it definitely couldn't make it any worse. "Sure."

I followed Mr. Ferris into the kitchen, where he maneuvered past a stack of moving boxes to get to the refrigerator. "I haven't packed any of the glasses yet, if you want one," he said, handing me an amber bottle.

"Don't need one." I looked around the spacious kitchen as I twisted off the cap and tried to imagine myself living here.

It wasn't a stretch. This was a nice, very livable house that any reasonable person not named Marietta Moreau should be able to feel at home in.

Since a blender and a stainless steel toaster appeared to be occupying the same space on the tile countertop as the last time I was here, I lifted the open flap of one of the cardboard boxes to see what sort of items Mr. Ferris was taking to the new abode. Assuming Marietta would let him take any.

"It's empty," he said, making me feel a little guilty for snooping. "I thought it was a bit premature to box everything up."

Made sense. "Because you won't be moving until after the honeymoon."

He gave me an easy grin. "Because I didn't know what you'd need."

Oh.

I sat on a barstool at the counter. "About that. I'm perfectly fine with staying at my apartment—"

"Now who's bending the truth a little?"

"Okay, not forever. But for now, it meets my needs."

"What if your mother and I prefer that you live here?"

I watched him as he took a swig of beer. "Are you sure this is something you're completely comfortable with, because if you aren't—"

Mr. Ferris held up his hand. "It will make your mother happy, and if she's happy, I'm okay with it."

Even though he seemed to be telling the truth, I wasn't entirely buying it.

"And like you said, this isn't forever," he added with a twinkle in his eye.

That I could buy. "Maybe try this for a year and see how we both feel about it?"

"Fine."

"And I'm paying you rent. Same as what I'm paying for my apartment."

"Your mother won't like that."

"Then don't tell her. This will be between you and me." I held up my beer bottle. "Is it a deal?"

He clinked it as if we had just made a toast. "You've got yourself a deal."

Chapter Twenty-Seven

"I STILL DON'T understand the secrecy about the house," Marietta said for the second time since we'd sat down for dinner with Gram and Steve. "If you and Barry reached some sort of agreement, why can't the rest of us hear about it?"

The moment that Marietta asked me for the ride home, I should have realized that she wouldn't stop pecking at me like a vulture until she had the whole story.

But I was well aware that she wouldn't like the twist I had added to her script. "Like I told you in the car, this is between Barry and me. All you need to know is that he and I have agreed that I'll move in after you two get back from your honeymoon and move into the new house."

"Well, I think that's excellent news," Gram stated, sounding every bit the head of the family. "And should be the last word on that subject."

"Your granny's laying down the law," Steve muttered in my ear. "I like it."

Me too, because I had more important things to think about than my mother's bruised ego.

While I dug into the chicken marsala rapidly cooling

on my plate, I glanced up to see Marietta frowning as much as her chemically treated brow would allow.

"You shouldn't encourage Barry to keep secrets from me," she stated. "That's the sort of thing that can really damage a relationship."

So could telling her that neither Mr. Ferris nor I wanted to follow Ted Skerrett's lead and have a sugar mama give us a free ride.

Gram gave her daughter the parental *look*. "Remember our talk about being a drama queen? Knock it off."

Thank you, Gram! "Besides, I was talking to Barry privately because he's the one who's going to be my landlord. Not you."

Marietta wagged her fork at me. "That's a temporary technicality and you know it. Because once Barry and I are married, what's his will be mine and vice versa."

"So you want to be the one I call when the water heater starts leaking?" I asked her. "Or when the oven element dies."

Her eyes widened. "What's an oven element?"

I reached for my wineglass. "I rest my case. Just be happy that we're both getting a house upgrade."

"Oh, speaking of cases," Gram said to me as I took a sip. "Did anything come of the rich widow theory we talked about the other day?"

I almost choked on my drink.

"And what theory would that be?" Steve asked nonchalantly.

I could feel my cheeks burning. "It's just an idea of Lucille's that we were kicking around."

"Having to do with Ted Skerrett's sudden interest in Winnie Dearborn right before he died," Gram added.

"But I thought Alice had a hand in coming up with the wealthy widow connection. Wasn't that what she told us when she and Duke were here?"

Steve's gaze pierced me like a shard of obsidian. "For a family meeting?"

I nodded.

"You had a family meeting without me?" Marietta protested.

Good grief. It wasn't bad enough that Steve knew that I had lied to him that night without her stirring more grievance into the mix? "You were a little preoccupied with cancelling your wedding at the time."

She vented a breath. "You could have filled me in. No matter what, I am still a member of this family."

"Honey, it was just about Ted Skerrett," Gram said to her daughter. "You remember him? Married my friend Ruth about twenty years ago?"

Marietta blinked. "Wasn't it Ruth's funeral that you went to several weeks back?"

"Yes, and Char just wanted to ask us a few questions. Sort of as background into the matter of his death." Gram turned to me. "That was pretty much the size of it. Right, honey?"

If I could have disappeared into my wineglass to escape the intensity of the stare from the detective next to me, I would have. "Pretty much."

"Just when did this matter become an open coroner case?" Steve asked.

There was no answer that I could provide that wouldn't result in him looking like he might spontaneously combust at my grandmother's dining table, so I reached out to touch his hand. "I can explain later."

He moved his hand to the napkin on his lap. "I don't think there's any explaining why you keep lying to me."

"I'm not! I just haven't told you the things I know you won't want to hear."

His mouth drew back into a humorless smile. "Yeah. Big difference."

"Children," Gram warned. "Let's not raise our voices at the table."

"Sorry, Eleanor." Scowling at me, Steve whispered, "You *will* explain later."

"There, that's better," she announced with satisfaction. "Now, who's ready for dessert?"

Not me. My stomach was already full with nervous knots.

Ten minutes after we finished the dishes, I was pacing the length of Steve's living room as I filled him in on everything I had uncovered to substantiate the rich widow theory.

Okay, almost everything. I left out the part about Grace Ivie being the one to clue me into the value of the lacquer box because I didn't want to get her into any trouble.

"So, when Ted set out for the trail, he thought his money problems were gonna be solved," I said, coming to a stop in front of the sofa, where Steve was staring at what was happening on his flat screen.

He glanced up at me as if I'd had too much of the marsala wine sauce. "And you, Lucille, Alice, and God knows who else think that Winnie pushed him off that overlook."

"No! Not Winnie, but it's possible that someone he'd had his sights on those last few days might have caught on that he really only wanted her for her money."

With a crack of a bat, Steve's focus shifted back to the Mariners game in progress. "Uh-huh."

I stepped in front of the TV. "That's all you have to say?"

"No, you're in the way."

"I'd like you to take this seriously, because I'm pretty much convinced that someone was up there with Ted that night."

Steve folded his arms as he tried to look around me. "Oh, I have no doubt that's what you think."

"Steve, what if someone was? There were two cars in the parking area that I haven't been able to account for, so... It's possible, right?"

"Anything's possible, Chow Mein. *Probable* is another matter entirely."

In other words, while he didn't want to dash my hopes on the rocks, he also didn't want to raise them. Which got me absolutely nowhere.

"What does Frankie think about this theory of yours?" he asked.

"I told her about the 'treasure' discovered in the house, but when she didn't seem especially interested in it, I didn't mention anything else. Until some real evidence got uncovered, it didn't seem like there was much point."

"Doesn't sound like you've found any."

I shook my head. "Without witnesses, it's all speculation."

Meeting my gaze, his mouth stretched into a hint of a

smile. "You're absolutely right, Deputy."

This was one time I wished I wasn't so right. "I don't know what to do."

Steve extended his arms in invitation and I climbed onto the sofa to snuggle next to him. "Maybe that's because there isn't anything to do but stop spinning those wheels, like we've talked about."

"Maybe."

"I've found that the key to that is to occupy your mind with something else."

I snuggled closer and nuzzled his neck. "I think I could do that."

"Good." Steve turned up the volume of the game. "Because the Mariners are about to load the bases."

That meant that I wouldn't be the one scoring anytime soon. "Swell."

Almost six hours later, I awoke to a thud. At first I thought it was Fozzie, but he was lying at the foot of my bed and growling at the wall.

"It's okay, boy," I said, rolling over. "It's just our noisy neighbors. We'll be rid of them soon."

Fozzie huffed as if he wasn't so sure I'd made the right decision about Mr. Ferris's house.

"It'll be fine." Despite my mother's irritation with me for not following the specifications of the plan she had laid out, everyone got something they wanted out of the deal.

Most important, my dog got a fenced yard.

"I don't know why she had to get so huffy about us

keeping a secret from her." I yawned. "Full disclosure can lead to some messy consequences."

True with Marietta.

True with Rox back when I wasn't ready to tell her about Steve and me.

And certainly true with Steve these last few months.

Although if I had mentioned meeting Ian and his daughter at the dog park earlier, I could have saved myself some grief.

Cute kid, I thought, my mind wandering as my eyelids drifted shut.

Cute dad, too.

It couldn't have been easy for the guy, that talk he had with his mom.

About something that she had been keeping a secret.

Winnie said that, right?

He didn't know at first.

I opened my eyes, staring into the darkness as my mind raced.

If he didn't know...

"Holy smokes!" I needed to talk to Ian.

Chapter Twenty-Eight

AFTER FOZZIE AND I took a quick walk in the early morning mist, I blasted my frizz into submission, swiped on some mascara, and had to dance a tango around the dog shadowing me as I ran from the bathroom to the kitchen to fill an insulated cup with coffee.

Credit where credit is due, my fur ball is pretty intuitive and can tell when something's brewing aside from the contents of my beeping coffee maker.

Okay, my mad dash to get out the door was giving him a big clue that his human had somewhere important to go. But what I hadn't expected when I gathered up my tote was that Fozzie would be pacing the entryway, insisting to come with me.

"No, you don't need to go," I said, nudging him out of the way. But I did. It was almost six, and while I had looked up the hours of Ian's veterinary clinic to confirm it didn't open until eight, if I wanted to be sure to catch him before he hit the road, I needed to leave now.

Fozzie woofed at me.

"I mean it. You're not going."

As I reached for the doorknob, he whimpered.

"It's not like I'm expecting any trouble. It's Ian."

The guy I had once suspected of killing Ted.

"Fine!" I grumbled, grabbing Fozzie's leash. "You big baby."

As soon as I opened the door, Fozzie charged ahead as if I hadn't been referring to him.

And maybe I wasn't entirely.

Twenty minutes later, parked on the street in front of Winnie's red brick Tudor, I was having trouble seeing out of the windows because Fozzie's panting was fogging them up.

I cracked open his window. "Sheesh, dog, just because I'm a little nervous doesn't mean that you have to be."

Sitting up on the passenger seat, he whimpered again.

Just as I reached to stroke his ear, I saw movement in the distance in front of me. A tall figure, approaching in a fluorescent vest the color of key lime pie—a jogger who looked to be as interested in me as I was in him.

I stepped onto the pavement with Fozzie scrambling out behind me. With a tight grip on the leash to keep him from dragging me past the relative safety of my car, I waved at Ian Dearborn.

He lifted his hand in greeting as he walked the last twenty feet to my car, his watchful eyes cutting to the dog tugging at his leash. "What're you doing here? Something wrong with Fozzie?"

"No, nothing like that. I just needed to talk to you about something and it couldn't wait."

Ian inched toward his mother's driveway. "Do you want to come in and have some coffee?"

"No, thanks." I didn't want Winnie to overhear our

conversation. I also didn't want her to look out her front window and see us, so I pointed down the street. "Since it's not raining at the moment, do you mind if we walk for a few minutes?"

Ian offered me a polite, tight-lipped smile as he adjusted his crimson Washington State University ball cap. "No problem. What's this about?"

"I don't know if your mom mentioned it, but I stopped by last week to talk to her about her relationship with Ted Skerrett."

Ian abruptly stopped. "How would that be any of your—"

"I'm a deputy coroner for the county, and I had to speak with everyone who had contact with Ted the day he died," I said while Fozzie pulled me a couple of steps closer to the dogwood he wanted to water.

"I get it." Ian smirked. "I thought it was a little too coincidental that you mentioned Spirit Rim at your appointment."

There was no point in denying my motive that day. "Sorry, I was just trying to get a sense of how much you knew—"

"About what?"

"About what happened to Ted."

"How would I know anything about that?" Ian asked, raising his voice as he loomed over me.

Stepping in front of me, Fozzie growled low in his throat.

I patted my protector's back. "It's okay, boy. Ian and I are just talking."

"And I'm sorry for being a little sneaky," I said to the guy looking at me as if I were as low as the dog pee at the base of that tree. "It's just that there are some things that have come up to suggest that Ted's death was no accident." Mainly from Lucille, so I sure hoped Ian wouldn't ask me to name my sources.

"What's that got to do with my mother?"

"Possibly nothing. But since she turned down his marriage proposal that day, it struck me that I should ask you what made her decide to do that on Friday of all days."

While Fozzie strained at the leash to resume our walk, Ian didn't move. Instead, he gave me a hard stare. "What'd she tell you?"

"Just that you voiced some concern about Ted."

"Then you already have your answer."

"Not entirely." Because I was missing one crucial piece of this puzzle. "You didn't know Ted personally, did you?"

Ian shook his head. "I only knew *of* him because my mom and his late wife were close friends."

"So what prompted you to have that 'awkward conversation' that you told me about?"

"I learned what the heck he was up to," Ian said, his volume increasing.

Clearly not from his mother. "Who told you?"

"Nadine..."

Holy crap!

"Sorry, I don't know her last name. She's one of my mother's friends from her exercise class." He pointed back the way we came. "Beyond that, I don't have much else I can tell you and need to wrap this up if I want to make it to the clinic on time."

I didn't need anything else, except to maybe mention

the one other item I'd been keeping from him. "I hope we're still on for Sunday. Now that Donna is taking care of Pumpkin, I thought she might like to join us and get acquainted with the dog park." *And you.*

Ian shot me another smirk as he leaned down to bury his hands in Fozzie's ruff. "That wouldn't have been because you were afraid to be alone with me, would it, Charmaine?"

"Of course not." Not now, at least.

"Uh-huh. See you Sunday, Fozzie Bear," Ian said, just before slanting me a sidelong glance from under the brim of his cap. "You too, you big chicken."

I glared at his rather attractive backside while he jogged toward the house. "I beg your pardon!"

Without looking back, Ian waved, and the racing heart of my inner fifteen-year-old skipped a beat.

Good grief.

"Come on," I said, leading Fozzie to the car. "We need to get you home." *And away from dangerously appealing men.*

And I needed to get to the courthouse to run a background check on Nadine Grunfeld.

Completing a search of the regional database two hours later, I hadn't discovered so much as a blemish on Nadine's record.

"Okay," I said, entering her name to see what the internet could tell me.

After scanning a short list of results composed mainly of phone and address records, I saw that she had previously lived in Port Townsend, and prior to that, a few locations in northern California. So Nadine had moved around a lot prior to settling down in Port Merritt. Big deal. I'd moved a few times, too, and was about to move again.

Two of these public information sites listed her as being related to a Lyle Grunfeld, so I searched for him and found only the one Port Townsend address that they had shared in common. Ancient history that reflected a marriage that didn't last that long. Unfortunately, that was something else that Nadine and I had in common, but pretty much what I had expected since I had once overheard her commiserating with one of the other waitresses at Duke's that she had married too young.

What I didn't find was any link to Ted. No addresses in common. No apparent shared history.

But Nadine had clearly formed some strong opinions about Ted—so strong that she warned Ian about him.

Because of something Ruth had confided in her?

If that had been the case and Ruth had regretted placing her trust in Ted, she wouldn't have left him the bulk of her estate.

No, it had to have been something that Ted did or said that caused Nadine to believe that she needed to protect Winnie against him.

I shut down my browser and called Duke's Gossip Central—my much more reliable information source.

"Duke's Cafe," my great-uncle answered after three rings.

"It's Char. Is Nadine Grunfeld there right now?"

"Yeah, the hens are at their corner table cackling as usual."

"Tell Lucille not to let her leave."

"The gals haven't even had their first coffee refill yet, so I don't think she's going anywhere soon. Now, if you don't mind," he said adding a dramatic pause worthy of my mother, "one of us has work to do."

Actually two of us, I thought as I dashed down the hallway with my tote. But I didn't have a clue how I was going to convince the hall monitor giving me the death stare that I had any urgent business to conduct at Duke's.

"Going somewhere, Charmaine?" Patsy asked with an icy calm that sent my pulse into hyperdrive.

"I ..." I looked for something, anything I could use as an excuse and spotted Shondra talking to her legal assistant.

"Shondra has something for me." And if she didn't, I was going to have to throw myself on her mercy and beg for her cooperation.

"Come back when you're done." Patsy's lips curled into a knowing smile. "I have a small copying project for you."

Oh joy.

Unfortunately, when Shondra saw me coming, she aimed a full-on scowl at me. "Girl, you'd better not be bringing me any trouble because I'm full up."

"Uh...I need to talk to you about a little development."

Stomping into her office like she wanted to drop-kick someone into space, Shondra sighed. "That's my life lately, little developments."

"Sorry to add one more," I said, standing in front of her desk as she took a seat. "But I think I've found a witness who can provide some new information about Ted Skerrett."

Shondra hung her head. "Why are we talking about this again?"

"Because I just found out that she was the one who got Mrs. Dearborn to break up with Ted."

"This isn't high school. In this office, we don't care who broke up with whom."

"I know, but..." I didn't have anything but a hinky feeling about Nadine. Was it because she had clearly been withholding information? Not only from me, but from Lucille and Carmen, and most important, from Winnie. "This woman, Nadine Grunfeld, knows a lot more than she's been telling, and I'd like to know why."

"Not everyone likes to talk to people as much as you seem to, Charmaine."

Jeez, Shondra was starting to sound like Steve. "She's over at Duke's Cafe right now, so—"

"You'd like to race right over and put her to your lie detector test."

I nodded.

After murmuring a few choice curse words, she shooed me away. "Go. But don't stay over there all morning. I don't need to get Patsy on my case."

"Yes, ma'am."

"And bring me back one of those apple fritters," Shondra called after me as I raced past her assistant's desk.

"Yes, ma'am!" If this went the way I hoped it would, I might even celebrate with one myself.

"Are you gonna tell us what's going on?" Alice asked when the kitchen back door clicked shut behind me.

Not yet. "I just need to talk to somebody. You know, see if something a witness told me checks out."

My great-aunt nodded. "Like a good investigator should. Steve better watch out, or he'll find himself out of a job pretty soon."

Nice to hear, but I was quite sure Steve wouldn't have been able to stop laughing if he'd been within earshot.

I tucked my tote into my locker and pulled an apron from a nearby rack.

Duke glowered at me as I stepped up to the pass-through window to see who was sitting with Nadine. "If Lucille sees you wearin' that apron she's gonna think you're after her tips."

I only had one tip for my favorite waitress: Stay away from Nadine's table.

Stanley looked over his newspaper as I headed for the coffee station where Lucille was brewing a fresh pot. "Did they run out of things for you to do at the courthouse?" he asked.

Sidling up next to Lucille, I pasted an innocent smile on my face. "It was a little slow, so I thought I'd come over and help out."

While Stanley grunted his skepticism, Lucille's pale brows furrowed. "Duke said something about the girls needing to stay until you got here," she whispered. "What's up?"

"Maybe nothing." I picked up the coffee carafe. "But if I'm able to get Nadine alone, don't come over."

Her furrow deepened. "Okay. As long as you fill me in later."

"Deal," I said, not knowing if I could keep up my end

of the bargain as I approached the corner table, where Carmen and Sylvia were cackling with glee while Winnie and Nadine looked bemused, as if they didn't get the joke.

I suspected that was because they hadn't been in a joking mood since Ian had that talk with his mom. "Morning, ladies."

Carmen smiled at me while I filled her cup. "What happened? Did Duke press you into service?"

I gave her a friendly wink. "Something like that."

"How's your grandmother, Char?" Sylvia asked. "We missed her at mahjong the other night."

"She's fine," I said, making my way around the table. "With my mother's wedding coming up, Gram just has a lot going on."

I refilled Nadine's cup last. "In fact, she wanted me to ask your advice about something."

Nadine's eyes widened. "*My* advice?"

I leaned over so that only she could hear me. "I wonder if we could talk in private for a moment."

After she exchanged glances with Winnie, Nadine pushed back her chair. "Of course."

Motioning to Lucille, I handed her the carafe. "Thanks." *Do not even think about squeaking in my direction.*

When she turned away without any glib commentary, I figured my message had been received.

So far, so good. But the hard part had yet to begin.

I gave Nadine what I hoped would be an encouraging smile and led her to the back corner of the diner, where the other ladies wouldn't be able to see us.

Equally important, no one was around to overhear.

"Thanks for doing this. Gram hasn't known who to turn to about this, but I thought you might be able to help us."

"I'm happy to help if I can," she said as we took seats across from one another.

"It's about the wedding. We have some concerns."

For a second it appeared as if Nadine had stopped breathing. "Concerns?"

"You know who my mother is."

The crow's feet at the corners of Nadine's eyes deepened. "I think so. Some sort of actress, right?"

Marietta wouldn't be happy to hear herself characterized that way, but it was close enough to suit my purposes. "Right, and she's engaged to someone nowhere near her pay grade, so my grandmother's concerned that my mom could be making a big mistake by rushing forward with this wedding."

"I see," Nadine said.

"So I thought I should ask how you handled it."

"I—I don't think I know what you mean."

Her deer in the headlights expression told me otherwise. "You know, when Ted started coming on so strong with Winnie. You owed it to her to say something, right? To clue her in that he was more interested in her money."

Nadine's nostrils flared as if she couldn't get enough oxygen. "I...didn't. I mean...not with Winnie. I—"

"I know. You told Ian instead."

Biting her lip, she closed her eyes.

"And of course, Winnie is broken-hearted, but it's better than Ted taking advantage of her, right?"

Nadine didn't move.

"I imagine she would have figured it out eventually. I mean, it's not like Ted hasn't had a preference for a certain kind of lady."

The flush creeping into Nadine's cheeks answered for her.

"Or am I wrong about that?" I asked.

Cocking her head, she grimaced as if the picture in her mind had caused her physical pain. "Not entirely."

That's when I saw it—the ache of regret etched across her face.

Oh. "You were in love with him."

With tears trickling down her cheeks, Nadine glanced out the window. "Once upon a time."

But clearly their relationship hadn't had a fairy tale ending. "But you knew he wouldn't marry you."

Instead of answering, she reached for a napkin and blotted her eyes.

"I take it that you didn't have all the qualities Ted was looking for in a wife."

"Hardly."

"But Ruth and Delia did."

No response.

"Well, he won't be marrying anyone now," I said to see if it would touch a nerve.

Nadine met my gaze, and the satisfaction that crept into the steely set to her jaw sent a shiver down my spine.

Oh, my. Not the reaction I was expecting to see.

And heaping on to the list of what I hadn't expected, I saw Winnie peering around the corner with her order ticket in hand.

That had to mean that this morning's gathering of

the Gray Ladies was breaking up. But I needed the lady sitting across from me to stick around, at least for another few minutes.

"We're almost done," I told Winnie, hoping that she'd get the hint.

Surprisingly, Nadine turned to give her friend a reassuring smile. "Are you heading home?"

"I thought I might go to the library first. I can wait for you if you'd like to come with me," Winnie said.

Nadine waved her off. "You go ahead. I'll catch up if I can."

That sounded like a big *if* to me, and the instant that Winnie disappeared from view, so did Nadine's smile. "We don't seem to be talking about your mother anymore."

"No. That's because Barry Ferris is very much alive."

She folded her hands in front of her and sighed.

Looking past Nadine, I watched Winnie climb into the ice-blue SUV parked on the street out front. "She tells you everything, doesn't she?"

"Who? Winnie?"

I nodded.

"I don't think she keeps many secrets from me, if that's what you mean."

That was exactly what I meant. "So you knew she had been taking all these long walks with Ted."

"Not at first," Nadine said with a deadly calm, staring down at the scarred surface of the table.

Yep, she knew. "But she told you about it. She needed to talk to someone. Who else would she turn to?" *Right?*

"She sure wouldn't tell Carmen. That old fool was determined to be the next Mrs. Skerrett. I should have told her she was wasting her time."

I saw an opportunity.

I could be reading this all wrong, but I felt like this was a now-or-never moment to find out if Nadine had wanted to say much the same thing to Ted that night.

"Instead, you made sure that there wouldn't be a next Mrs. Skerrett," I said, locking onto Nadine's gaze. "Unless you want to tell me it was an accident."

She winced, her eyes pooling. "I think I may need a lawyer."

"Yep." *Me, too.*

I grabbed my phone to call Shondra.

Chapter Twenty-Nine

AFTER DETECTIVE PEARSON showed up to take Nadine in for questioning at the county jail, I spent the next six hours waiting for Shondra to bring back some news.

Finally, after Patsy left the office around five-thirty I figured I'd better do the same before my hungry dog decided to chew up the carpet and cost me the damage deposit I was hoping to get back next month.

That's when I saw a weary-looking Shondra limping toward her office as if she'd been on her feet most of the day.

"Well?" I asked, following her down the hall. "Did Nadine confess?"

"Once her attorney and I were able to convince her she could save herself a lot of prison time, yeah. She started talking."

To save herself prison time? "She copped a plea?"

Dropping her briefcase by her desk, Shondra fell into her chair and shot me a sardonic look. "Steve's right. You watch too much TV."

I saw no reason to stand there and be insulted, so I took a seat with the hope that she would elaborate.

"Then maybe you'd like to explain what you mean to this civilian."

"Quickly, 'cause I need to write the charging document, and my husband is already unhappy with me after being home most of the day with a sick kid. In short, Ms. Grunfeld decided to 'fess up and explain how Skerrett tumbled into that ravine. It was either that or look at the possibility of spending the rest of her life in an orange jumpsuit."

I scooted to the edge of my chair. "So Nadine really did kill him?"

"Not intentionally. From her account, Ms. Grunfeld knew from her friend when he'd likely be hitting that trail, so when she spotted his Caddy parked—"

"But Mr. Skerrett's stepchildren didn't mention seeing her when they were there. Did she say what time this was?"

"I think she said around six. She'd been babysitting and had to wait for her daughter to get home from the store."

"So she would have just missed them." Because Marc had had that call of nature and insisted on leaving.

"Detective Pearson will speak to those two again to corroborate their stories, but it seems that we still don't have any witnesses to what happened up there. What we do have is a remorseful lady who admits that the chat she wanted to have with her old boyfriend got out of hand."

"So this was an accident?" Because that glint of satisfaction I had seen on Nadine's face had suggested otherwise.

"Not that simple. Because she didn't consider his

safety in light of the slick conditions, where they were standing, and of course the consequences of the shove she gave the dude to cause him to stumble off that overlook. So unless Frankie takes exception with it, that's Man-two."

Manslaughter. "Yikes." That would still amount to several years in prison.

What I hadn't heard yet was what had led to that fateful moment. "Did Nadine explain why things got physical? I know she'd had good reason to be angry with him."

Shondra's gaze sharpened. "You didn't mention that you knew about that."

I wasn't sure that we were talking about the same thing. "I meant him targeting her best friend. Between her history with Mr. Skerrett and everything that Winnie was telling her..."

Shondra pulled a file from her briefcase. "Ahh. There was that, too."

Too? "What are you referring to?"

"Skerrett's 'Oh baby, you know you've always been the only one for me' act now that he thought he was gonna be rich."

"He told her about that Japanese art treasure that the appraisers found at the house?"

"No." Shondra frowned at me as if I were about to be grounded. "And how could you possibly know about that?"

I shrugged. "Lucky guess?"

"I swear," she said, shaking her head. "You poke your nose in more places where it doesn't belong."

"I like to think of it as being thorough."

"Right." Shondra's mouth flat-lined as she jotted a note in the file. "Well, *Ms. Thorough*, Pearson's gonna want to talk to you too, so expect a call. And try not to say anything to make me regret sending you out there to talk to the sister in the first place."

"Yes, ma'am." That would be my plan.

"So are we done? I've got stuff to do."

"I guess." But now that I had the answers that I had been searching for since the morning Ted's body was discovered, his final moments seemed all the more tragic.

Shondra looked up from her notes. "I don't see you moving."

"I was just thinking about Mr. Skerrett. Those last couple of hours of his life ... he must've thought he had it made."

"Yeah, he told Ms. Grunfeld that his ship had come in ... that they'd be able to sail away together." Shondra wrinkled her nose. "If he'd fed that piece of crap line to me, I might've socked him one myself. Not that I'm saying I would've wanted the guy to take a header into the ravine. But considering that Nadine showed up out of the blue so that she could tell him off, he chose a piss-poor time to act like the contemptible jerk that he was."

"Ouch," Steve said from the doorway. "Hope you're not talking about me."

Shondra slanted an irritated glance at him. "Not anymore, we're not. And you'd better not be here wanting anything official from me, 'cause I've had enough for one day."

"You and me both." Steve took a couple of steps toward me. "I'm just here to pick up the birthday girl."

I sucked in a breath. "Oh my gosh, I forgot all about it."

"Just how do you forget your own birthday?" Shondra asked me.

"I guess I was a little preoccupied."

Steve pressed his palm to the small of my back. "If you're done being preoccupied, can we go now?"

Shondra waved us toward the door. "Yes. Go so I can finish this."

"Thanks for the info," I said, looking back over my shoulder. "I don't think I would have been able to sleep tonight without knowing the rest of the story."

"You done good." Shondra's lips curled into a begrudging smile. "You can be a real pain in the butt sometimes, but you done good."

I was standing in her doorway reveling in her backhanded compliment when the phone in my tote bag started ringing. "Oh, that reminds me. What was Mr. Skerrett doing with that cell phone? Since there was no service out there—"

"Nadine mentioned that he had an app on his phone—some sort of step tracker that he kept looking at while she was trying to get his undivided attention. Let that be a lesson to you, Detective," Shondra said, calling out to Steve in the hallway. "Keep your dang phone in your pocket tonight or there could be trouble."

I grinned at him. "Yeah!"

"There *will* be trouble if we don't get out of here pretty soon," he grumbled.

"Go," Shondra said. "Have a happy birthday and let me get some work done."

I linked my arm with Steve's. "You heard the woman.

Let's go."

Halfway down the hall, I stopped in my tracks. "Let me just check my phone. That might have been Donna or Rox wanting to meet up for my birthday."

"About that—"

"Nope," I said when I saw the number for the missed call. "It was just my mother. It's strange that no one has texted or called me all day. I know it's pretty bad to forget my own birthday, but did everyone else forget too?"

Steve took my hand and led me to the door. "No one forgot."

I put the brakes on. "What are you saying?"

"Everyone's waiting for you at your granny's house."

"A surprise party?"

"Sort of your mother's idea that I tried to discourage, but I don't think my vote counted."

I cringed. "This is what she cornered you about when you gave her that ride to Mr. Ferris's house."

Steve held the door open for me. "She wanted to do something special for you after everything you've done to help her with the wedding."

"Crap. I hate surprise parties."

He gave me a little push through the door. "She's called me twice in the last half hour to ask what's keeping you."

I groaned. "Sorry. I just need to get home and feed Fozzie and then we can go."

"Already done."

"You walked him, too?"

"Yep, so no excuses. We're going now."

"Swell."

"And Chow Mein?"

Hoping he wouldn't give me any more bad news, I looked up at him.

He planted a kiss on my lips. "Happy birthday."

✻

Two days later, I was in a Rainshadow Ridge Resort changing room glaring at the wrinkles in my peach chiffon bridesmaid dress when I heard a knock at the door.

"How're you doing in there?" Steve asked.

I opened the door to let him in. "I'm wrinkled."

He inspected my face. "Hey, it's not like we're eighteen anymore."

This wasn't what I needed right now. "I meant my dress."

"Oh. Can't help you with that either, Chow Mein."

Stepping to the doorway, I scanned the crowd gathering near the white tent that had been set up should the morning's showers make a comeback. "Is Donna out there somewhere?"

"Busy next door doing your mom's hair."

I ran a hand over the stiff plaited up-do that Donna had shellacked into place in case the wind picked up. "No doubt with a full can of hairspray."

"How about Rox?" She'd been a bridesmaid many times over. She had to know something about getting wrinkles out of chiffon.

"Haven't seen her for a while," Steve said, looking so relaxed and debonair in the black tuxedo he threw on ten minutes earlier that it seemed unfair. "Do you want me to hunt her down for you?"

"Don't bother." I turned to the mirror mounted opposite the door to try to smooth out the major wrinkle in the back of my dress. "It's not like anyone will be looking at me anyway."

Noticing Steve smiling at my reflection, I checked my teeth to make sure I hadn't smeared them with mocha-flavored lip gloss. "What?"

"I didn't say anything."

"Yeah, but you look like you want to say something."

Just as he opened his mouth, the pint-sized wedding planner who had herded us into these changing rooms when we arrived an hour earlier rapped on the open door. "Five minutes. Maid of honor, groomsman, are we ready?"

"We're ready," Steve answered for me as the woman scurried next door to call on the much more important member of the wedding party—the bride.

I took one last look in the mirror. The poofy dress made me feel like I was swishing around in peach meringue, but at least it fit. "Mission accomplished, I guess. What do you think?"

His gaze raked over me. "Do you really need to hear how good you look?"

Well... "Yes."

"Okay. Then you look nice."

"*Nice!* Nice is all you got for me after I let my mother take a full hour to do my makeup? Do you realize how much—"

"Gotcha," Steve said with a grin.

"You're a jerk."

He gave me a lingering glance from the doorway. "I

love you, too. See you out there."

A second later, he was gone. "Wait! What?"

THE END

About the Author

Wendy Delaney writes fun-filled cozy mysteries and is the award-winning author of the Working Stiffs Mystery series. A longtime member of Mystery Writers of America, she's a Food Network addict and pastry chef wannabe. When she's not killing off story people she can be found on her treadmill, working off the calories from her latest culinary adventure. Wendy lives in the Seattle area with the love of her life and has two grown sons.

For book news or to subscribe to Wendy's newsletter, please visit her website at www.wendydelaney.com. Email her at wendy@wendydelaney.com, and connect on Facebook at www.facebook.com/wendy.delaney.908.